OTHERLANDER

A Long Way From Home

T. KEVIN BRYAN

For Linda and Hayden

For we do not wrestle against flesh and blood, but against the rulers, against the authorities, against the cosmic powers over this present darkness…

Ephesians 6:12

Chapter 1

Daniel Colson trudged across the field. His coat, wet from the driving mist of the coming storm, whipped in the wind. Even this close, he still feared he might be too late.

Ominous clouds filled the night sky. They churned and boiled. Lightning flashed, followed by the deep roll of thunder.

Daniel stopped. Pulled the spectacles from his face to reveal deep blue eyes, like the churning ocean. His hair, tousled by the wind, was dark brown and streaked with gray at the temples, it gave him a scholarly look that helped with the more seasoned professors at the university. He wiped away the gathered moisture from the lenses. He peered back over his shoulder. From this distance, he could still make out the village's glow, peeking over the horizon.

At age thirty-seven, he was a man torn in two. One half was secured to this world, held fast by the anchor that was his family—a wife and their son. But it wasn't enough to overcome the rage he was feeling.

His other half was being driven relentlessly to take

back what was his, the years of research that was stolen from him.

Daniel didn't think of himself as a man of action, but a man of learning—an archeologist from Stanford University doing work at Edinburgh.

He replaced his spectacles. Adjusting the strap of his leather bag across his shoulder, he set his face into the stiff wind and marched steadily on.

It was miserable going now, as Daniel continued to trudge up the almost imperceptible rise in the landscape. He leaned into the wind, walked with greater determination.

Peering into the thick darkness, Daniel wondered if he'd lost his bearings—easy to do in this starless-night fog. A crack of lightning illuminated the surrounding landscape, and his final destination: huge monolithic stones standing black against the stormy sky.

Another flash revealed more hulking stones, some standing like giant rustic pillars, others like massive bowling balls left by the children of giants. They formed a full circle, like the apse of some ancient cathedral. In old Scotland, it was known as "Mairead Fhada." But the local folk today just called it "Long Meg and Her Daughters." It was one of over thirteen hundred stone circles scattered across Britain, Stonehenge was the most famous. Daniel knew it held secrets; ancient secrets for it had stood watch over this landscape for over thirty-five hundred years. It was those secrets that drew him to this land. It was their pull that caused him to uproot his family and move across the Atlantic.

Daniel dropped his leather bag to the ground, then searched through its contents: a couple of wrapped sandwiches, three reference books, his laptop computer. Beneath all that was what he was looking for—an ancient illuminated manuscript. He opened it to reveal pages of strange script. It was known as illuminated because each page had been decorated with drawings of scenes that shed light upon the pages contents. Also some of the letters were written with gold leaf that seemed to shine on the page.

His fingers ran the length of the page, searching. From inside his coat, he pulled a small leather notebook, worn smooth from years of use. He opened it, and the wind tore at the pages. He referenced his own hand-drawn sketches and diagrams and compared them to similar drawings in the ancient book.

The storm grew. Daniel felt that at any moment, the howling winds might sweep him away. With difficulty, he placed everything back in the bag but the notebook. He kept that out for reference.

Reshouldering the bag, Daniel looked to the most prominent stone of Mairead Fhada, the rock known as "Long Meg." She stood southwest outside the circle by about twelve paces. He checked his notes and then moved directly to the giant, silent monolith. At over twelve feet high and at least nine tons, the stone dwarfed him.

Daniel stopped in front of it, checked his position against his notes, then walked resolutely along the interior perimeter of the pillared circle. He slowed as he neared the third pillar on his traverse, checked his notebook, then stopped.

Another glance at his notes, then looking down to his left and his right. Yes, this is the starting point. Then, hesitantly, he took the next step.

Immediately, lightning struck that third stone. Daniel cringed but then was mesmerized as he watched the bolt, rather than receding into the stormy clouds, clutched the giant pillar in an eerie, electrical grip.

Finally tearing his gaze from the illuminated stone, he

looked back to his notes, then continued walking his precise pattern to the next rock, counting each step as he went. Crack! Lightning struck and held that stone, just like the previous one.

Daniel moved faster. He walked a loop to the center, then back out to another stone. As he passed each stone, a new bolt of lightning struck and held it. One after another, pulsing white tentacles of electricity reached from the clouds and haloed each of the stones.

He continued his cosmic dance with the stormy forces until lightning gripped every pillar and boulder. Finally, he froze at the very center of the ancient ruins, now glowing and white-hot under the electrical inverted umbrella. Outside the ruins, the storm raged on.

Daniel glanced from stone to stone. He could feel his skin prickling as the power of the storm roared. Then, through barely parted lips, he whispered, "Forgive me, Caroline."

At once, lightning streaked from every stone and struck Daniel. The lightning held him in its luminous grip and lifted him from the ground.

He screamed. But his scream was cut short by a massive surge of energy, and in a blinding flash that popped, he disappeared.

The energy dissipated. The electric arms of lightning receded into the dark heavens with faint crackles. Thunder echoed in the distance as the storm died.

Smoldering, the leather notebook lay open on the ground where Daniel last stood. The wind tore at the notebook's charred pages, and one by one, they scattered across the grass or were blown into the sky.

One frail page snagged on a stone, hung for a moment, then slipped to the ground, obscured between the monolith and the tall grass. It was the hand-drawn diagram of the stone circle known as Mairead Fhada.

Chapter 2

In a classroom at St. Vic's Academy, Thomas Colson sat uncomfortably in his gray school uniform. He was twelve. He had the green eyes of his mother and the brown hair of his father, which was now a scruffy mess. In the summer, back in his native California, his hair would turn almost blonde, bleached by the sun. Around him, his gray-uniformed classmates feverishly scratched out sentences on lined paper with their No. 2 pencils.

Thomas surveyed the classroom, subtly, to avoid arousing the attention of Mr. Fergus, his teacher, who stood ensconced against the room's back wall, hidden behind that day's edition of the newspaper, with only the great white mop of his hair visible.

Turning back to his own exam page, where he should've been writing his essay, Thomas instead began sketching a strange circular pattern. It was almost a replica of the diagram in Daniel Colson's notebook at Mairead Fhada.

After a few more pencil scratches, Thomas pulled absentmindedly at his uniform shirt's stiff collar. His gaze turned to look out the drop-sprinkled window near his desk. Drizzling. Always drizzling.

At home in America, Thomas would call this "mist." He wished it would either dry up or be a real proper rain. It seemed like all his time here in England was an in-between time.

Neither here nor there. The sky was neither black nor blue. Gray sky, gray clouds, gray land. Everything was gray. That's how he felt inside: gray and drizzling.

Smack! A paper-wad to the back of his head knocked Thomas out of his daydream. He reached down and uncrumpled the ball of paper, smoothing it on his desk. "YANK GO HOME!" was scrawled in big black letters.

Thomas's face flushed with anger. He glanced behind him. Everyone there was busily writing—except in the back corner. The boys there had their heads down snickering into their hands.

That's it, Thomas thought. *You picked the wrong day to pick on this "Yank!"* Thomas wadded the paper back into a tight ball. He glanced back where the boys were pretending to work, almost right under Mr. Fergus's newspaper. The teacher seemed to not have noticed at all.

This heartened Thomas. And so, despite him never having been much of a pitcher back home on his baseball team, he felt confident he'd at least hit one of the boys.

He continued squeezing the paper into a tight wad as he waited patiently for his moment. He didn't have to wait long. One of the boys poked his head up to take a peek in Thomas's direction.

"You're mine," whispered Thomas, and let the paper wad fly. At that exact moment, Mr. Fergus sensed something and glanced up over his newspaper.

Ssswhack! The projectile hit the man full in the face. Thomas spun and dove back into his essay. *Why me? Why does it always have to be me?* Thomas pretended to write as the whole class giggled.

Slowly, Thomas tugged his gaze up from his paper. Gray-flannel trousers standing at his desk filled his vision. Thomas looked up to face a very grim Mr. Fergus, clutching the paper wad in his fist.

"Mr. Colson... if you would kindly come with me?" Mr. Fergus said in his deep British accent.

Thomas stood and followed Mr. Fergus. As he did, the boys in the corner made faces and laughed.

Then, just before the reluctant Thomas was out of the room, he caught the eye of a round-faced boy with bright eyes behind spectacles. This was Pudge, and he was Thomas's only friend in the school. Pudge just grinned and shook his head in disbelief.

Chapter 3

Thomas sat on the large wooden bench outside the headmaster's office. The door opened and a voice from inside called, "Mr. Thomas Colson."

Thomas stood and took a deep breath, "Well, here we go."

As Thomas entered the headmaster's office, he imagined how its decorator must have been thinking, "Early hunting lodge meets antique library." Leather-bound books lined the shelves; animals' heads lined the walls.

One particularly vicious-looking wild boar stared at Thomas from the corner. Thomas thought, If he were here many more times, the headmaster would find a space to mount his head.

Thomas slid into the hard wooden chair across from the headmaster's desk, prepared for the worst. The headmaster adjusted his tweed jacket and pulled the pipe he never smoked from between his clenched teeth.

"Mr. Colson, I know you may not be with us much longer. But until you are gone, you could make your stay easier for us all by simply spending more time on your studies and less time launching projectiles at your fellow classmates."

"Yes, sir," said Thomas.

"I'm afraid I'll need to talk to your father about this."

Thomas stiffened.

"Sir, my dad is... uh, out of town... on business."

The headmaster looked long and hard at the boy. Thomas felt like he was under a microscope—no, not a microscope, an X-ray machine. Could he see? Thomas wondered, could he see through him? But even though Thomas's insides were churning, he held his face in sullen indifference.

Suddenly the headmaster snapped out of his X-ray mode, popped his pipe back between his teeth, and said with finality: "Right. Yes, of course. Well, your mother then."

Thomas cringed.

Chapter 4

The school bell rang, breaking the silence. The building's doors burst open, and a massive gray torrent of uniformed students came streaming out, laughing and yelling. Then the gray river turned to a trickle. Finally, one last student stepped through the doors: Thomas.

As he descended the school steps, Thomas untucked and unbuttoned his white-starched shirt like he couldn't stand to be in it one more second. This revealed a T-shirt emblazoned with his favorite superhero: Wolverine.

"Hallo, Thomas!" A voice called behind him.

Thomas turned to see Pudge, coming his way alone as the current of other kids had moved on.

"Hey, Pudge," Thomas mumbled.

The boys ambled away from the after-school ruckus.

Smiling, Pudge said, "That was pretty good pitching today. May I call you Mr. Baseball?"

Thomas's mood was not so easily lifted. "Those guys are jerks."

"How did it go with Chuckles?"

Thomas straightened to his full height, tilted his head,

cocked his eyebrow, and announced in his best English accent: "I must concentrate on my studies and refrain from launching projectiles." The boys shared a laugh.

"Come on!" exclaimed Pudge. "Today's the big game!"

"Pudge, you know how I hate this."

"I promised the chaps I would find someone to take Walter's position."

Thomas looked at Pudge. His mind was reeling. He seized at something to get him out of this: "I—I've got a lot of library research to catch up on!"

Pudge rolled his eyes—"Nice try!"—And gave Thomas a punch in the shoulder. "Thomas, you're a twelve-year-old lad. It's time you started actin' like it. And don't worry; they won't make you pitch."

Chapter 5

In the open field near the edge of St. Vic's campus, Thomas stood holding a cricket bat. Although the day was still cloudy and cold after the drizzle, Thomas wiped sweat from his forehead thinking, How did he get himself into these situations?

Arnie, the paper-wad thrower from class, stood in the pitcher's position. His school uniform was already rumpled and dirty from the game. Arnie glared at the pristine Thomas, and his face twisted into a malicious smirk.

Pudge sat in the grass on the sidelines and actually looked more nervous than Thomas. Pudge's eyes were wide, and his mouth hung open as if anticipating the candy bar he forgot he held.

Thomas looked at Pudge, eyes pleading for help.

"You can do it," Pudge mouthed silently.

Thomas turned his gaze back to the pitcher. *I can do this!* He thought. Then Arnie wound up expertly, took two quick steps, leaped into the air, and hurled the ball.

As the ball came speeding toward him, Thomas gritted his teeth and swung.

However, at the last moment, he closed his eyes... so the ball hit the wickets.

The schoolboys in the field jumped and cheered, then rushed to Arnie. They slapped him on the back and ruffled his hair.

Watching the rejoicing boys, Thomas just stood there, holding his bat limply. He turned to his own teammates. They all walked off, grumbling under their breath.

"Hey, guys," Thomas pleaded. They just kept walking. One or two looked back at Thomas, then shook their heads in disgust.

"Guys?"

"Don't worry, Thomas. They'll get over it." Pudge consoled him as he threw an arm around Thomas's shoulder.

"Hey, Thomas!"

Thomas and Pudge turned to see Arnie, surrounded by his rejoicing teammates.

"You ought to have your pop practice with you!" Arnie taunted. The boys all exploded into laughter, even as they continued leaving the field.

Thomas's eyes narrowed as he watched the boys leave. He tried to think of some smart, sarcastic comeback, but nothing came. He stood clenching his fists.

"Come on, Thomas," Pudge beckoned.

"No."

"They don't mean nothin' by it."

Pudge reached out his hand to restrain his friend, but he was too late.

Thomas flew across the field, and before Arnie had a chance to react, Thomas was on him, pummeling him with his fists like a windmill.

"Take it back!" Thomas screamed.

Despite the barrage, Arnie finally got a good punch in striking Thomas in the mouth and sent him flying.

Arnie scrambled to his feet, flanked by his teammates. "What's wrong with you, Colson?" He demanded and then rubbing his jaw turned and stomped away.

Thomas wiped his bloody lip and watched them go.

Chapter 6

Thomas and Pudge walked briskly up the cobbled street of their small English village, Little Salked. It was located in Cumbria a county in North West England. Thomas surveyed the stone cottages that hugged tightly to each other on both sides of the road. They were built of a hardy tan stone that was quarried from the land many hundreds of years ago. He often felt as if he was living in an episode of one of those British children's TV shows about a really useful steam engine.

Every few steps, Pudge glanced at Thomas. He knew his friend was angry but didn't know how to snap him out of it. Oh well, Pudge thought, might as well use the old traditional. He hauled off and punched Thomas on the shoulder.

"Hey!" exclaimed Thomas, grimacing and rubbing the sore spot. "What was that?"

"That was the T.O.T.," Pudge said matter-of-factly.

"And what, may I ask, is the T.O.T.?"

"The Old Traditional. I find it useful to knock young lads out of their sulking."

"Oh, really?"

"Yes, really! It is about time you snapped out of it. It's just a game. It's not that big a deal!"

At that, Thomas turned on Pudge.

"To you! You weren't the one up there. You weren't the one they were laughing at!"

Having realized he had struck a sore spot, Pudge just stammered, "Your lips bleeding again."

"Forget it." Thomas turned, wiped his lip, and started walking again. Leaving Pudge dumbfounded.

"Why do they call it cricket, anyway?" Thomas called back over his shoulder.

"I dunno," gasped Pudge as he ran to catch up.

"It's a bug."

"What?"

"A cricket's a bug. Who'd name a game after a stupid bug? Baseball makes sense. You got a base, you got a ball... baseball!"

"Huh, I never thought about it."

Thomas turned to Pudge and with a glint in his eye, said, "Well, while you're thinking about it, I'll race you to my house. Ready? Set? Go!" And he was off like a shot, flying up the sidewalk.

Pudge lumbered after him. "Hey, that's not fair!"

Chapter 7

Thomas sat in his father's old wooden office chair, staring at the screen of the desktop computer in his father's home office. Clearly, the room of a busy archaeology professor, its walls were covered with books and framed photographs of ancient digs around the world. Dusty artifacts cluttered the shelves. It was one of Thomas's favorite places to hang out.

Thomas studied a design on the computer monitor. A symmetrical symbol, an endless knot: three smooth and intertwined leaves seemingly looping back on themselves within a circle. Unity in diversity. To some it represented the Holy Trinity: A profound mystery only to be accepted by faith. As he accompanied his father on explorations in the Celtic lands of this ancient country, Thomas had seen this symbol carved on many crosses and at important archeological sites.

On the desk beside Thomas, a plate of cookies and two glasses of milk waited.

Thomas's concentration on the graphic circle was broken by heavy breathing. Pudge sagged in the office doorway, doubled over, holding the doorjamb for support and gasping for breath.

"What took you so long?" Thomas asked nonchalantly without taking his eyes from the computer screen.

"Thanks a lot," Pudge said, still gasping for breath. "You know I'm not as fast as you are."

Thomas ignored the comment and just motioned to the snacks. "Have some cookies."

At that, Pudge's exhaustion suddenly vanished; he stood straight up and blurted: "Mmm, cookies!" Pudge eagerly took the plate of cookies and a glass of milk.

With a sigh, he plopped into the large leather chair across from Thomas and began munching. "What's that?" Pudge managed, through his mouthful of cookies.

"What's what?"

"That thing on your computer."

Thomas swiveled in his father's old chair. "That," he said, "is a Celtic circle."

Pudge rolled his eyes. "I know it's a Celtic circle. What do you think I'm daft? I actually grew up around here. Why are you staring at it?"

"This one, I believe, is supposed to symbolize the Trinity. It's the last project my dad was working on. He thought it was somehow related to the stone circle outside of town, Mairead Fhada."

"You mean," Pudge held up his fingers, making air quotes. "Long Meg and her Daughters? That's what everyone around here calls it. What did you say your dad does?"

"Professor of archaeology," Thomas said as he swiveled the chair with a creak back toward the computer.

Thomas picked up a dog-eared book its pages sprouting yellow post-its.

Pudge read the dust jacket. "The Stone Circle En...ig...ma..."

"Enigma, Pudge. It means puzzle, mystery." Thomas called from behind the book.

"Sounds like an episode of Dr. Who." Pudge began to hum his best rendition of the famous British TV show's theme.

"Look at the author," Pudge exclaimed, chuckling, staring at the author's photo on the book jacket. He was a man in his thirties with a white beard and a very pale complexion. "That guy needs some serious sun!"

"He had a skin condition you goofball. He's the author, Dr. Michael Avery, He was Professor of Medieval Studies over at Edinburgh. He died when my dad was in college."

"Well, he gives me the creeps!"

"You are daft!"

Pudge thought on that for a moment. "Hmm, Hey! Let's go over to my house and play some video games."

"Not right now."

Pudge continued munching as he watched Thomas reading.

"Thomas, am I your best mate?" Pudge said to the back of the book.

"No," Thomas responded matter-of-factly.

"Why not?"

"I already have a best friend."

"Your dad?"

Thomas lowered the book.

"Yeah. You know, friends don't play all the time. Sometimes they have work to do."

Pudge let that sink in. Then he hesitantly asked, "Have you heard anything?"

Thomas stopped looking at the computer, turned to fix

his eyes on a photograph of himself and his father—Daniel, from an archeological site.

Thomas's mother took the photo when they were all on a dig in Israel. Daniel and Thomas were both smiling, and Thomas proudly held up a bit of dusty pottery.

Thomas remembered Pudge's question and said, "No."

"You think he's coming back?"

Thomas turned on Pudge. "What do you mean by that?"

Pudge realized he had crossed the line again. "Nothing... I don't mean anything. I was just asking if—"

"He's coming back," Thomas interrupted. "And I think it's time for you to go."

Reluctant, but catching Thomas's drift, Pudge stood and moved to the door.

"See you tomorrow?"

Thomas ignored his friend, just continued staring at the computer.

"Thomas?"

"Yeah."

"I hope he does. I hope he does come back."

Thomas softened a bit. "Yeah... thanks."

Chapter 8

Thomas lay prone on his bed, reading a text on his cell phone. It read: "Caroline and Thomas, I must go now—no time. Be back soon. Please forgive me! Love you, see you, keep the faith!"

How long had it been? Thomas thought. He slowly reread the note. "Love you, see you, keep the faith"? It was increasingly difficult to find any warmth or tenderness in his father's traditional salutation.

In fact, now, as Thomas reread the text, it just made anger rise in his heart. If my father really loved me, how could he leave me? Thomas squeezed his eyes shut, Trying not to allow the tears to spill onto his cheeks. They came anyway.

He peered up at a framed photo resting on his nightstand. It was one of his favorites, of much happier times. In it, Thomas stood smiling with his mother, an attractive blonde lady, and his father, Daniel Colson, in front of an old Irish castle.

Seeing the photo, reading the text, remembering the trouble at school—it all finally got the best of him.

Thomas flung the phone across the room, then balled up his fist and drove it into his pillow.

There was a knock at the door.

Thomas sat up quickly, wiped his face and tried to regain his composure. "Yeah?"

"Thomas, can I come in?" asked a woman's voice from the other side of the door.

"Yeah, Mom," Thomas remembered his busted lip and shielded it with his hand.

The door opened to reveal Caroline Colson, Thomas's mother. She was thirty-four, and her deep green eyes reminded Thomas of a clear lake reflecting the surrounding forest. They also revealed a mother who loved her son deeply.

As she sat on the edge of Thomas's bed, he knew her heart was still hurting. He felt ashamed of himself and his anger. Yes, he was missing his dad. But how must his mom feel? Her husband was gone, and to who knows where?

"You okay, honey?" Caroline asked.

"Uh-huh," Thomas replied without conviction.

Caroline nodded. "The headmaster called today. Is there something you want to talk about?"

"Not really," he mumbled, still hiding his injury.

Caroline reached gently and moved Thomas's hand from his mouth. Her eyes widened.

Silence filled the room, then she responded softly, "Okay... well, it's late... time to get ready for bed. Come down in a minute and I'll kiss you good night."

She stood and, giving him a little smile, walked out of the bedroom.

Caroline had only walked a few feet down the hall when she heard Thomas's voice:

"Mom?"

She turned with concern. Thomas stood at the edge of

the doorway. Even though he was almost as tall as her, she couldn't help but see him as her baby son, still small and vulnerable.

"Is Dad..." Thomas struggled to say the words. "Is he coming back?"

Caroline rushed to her son and wrapped him in a warm embrace. She couldn't hold back the tears as her heart broke for her son.

Caroline gave Thomas one more gentle squeeze. Then, grasping his shoulders, she looked deep into his eyes and said with as much confidence as she could muster, "He said he would. And your father always keeps his promises."

Chapter 9

Thomas reclined on the couch, ready for bed in his favorite soft sweatpants and old Wolverine shirt that was almost worn through.

Caroline walked out of the kitchen carrying a container of ice cream, and with a big flourish, exclaimed, "Ta-daa! Chocolate-chip-cookie dough."

Smiling, Thomas got up from the couch. "My favorite!"

"Get the spoons. Let's eat on the porch."

The night sky was brilliant with stars. Their cottage was situated on the outskirts of the small village of Little Salked a few miles from Penrith in Cumbria. Thomas's father had rented the cottage there because it was only a little over a mile to the stone circle, Mairead Fhada.

Thomas and Caroline sat on the front stoop, both wrapped in blankets, sharing ice cream out of the carton.

"This is one of the nice things about our stay here," Caroline said. "We didn't have this view back in the city."

Thomas pointed at the night sky and exclaimed: "Mom, look! There it is!"

Caroline noticed the star below Orion's belt twinkling brightly.

"Yes. The famous Bud's Star."

"Tell it to me again."

Thomas's mother gazed at him, under his big blanket. She sighed and began:

"Once upon a time, there was a knight who was the bravest in all the land. This knight was also brilliant. In fact, he went on a quest to seek knowledge at the most excellent university in the land."

"While on the path to a Ph.D., he discovered something else—love. And that love was the irresistible Princess Caroline, who swept that knight right off his feet."

Thomas chuckled at that.

Caroline continued: "Soon they were married. Then the knight became a professor, the princess became a writer, and on a cold winter night, they had a beautiful baby boy."

She leaned over and kissed Thomas on the top of his head.

"When they took him home, the knight and the princess held that little boy close and looked up at the stars. They picked out a star and made a wish, and the knight said: 'From this day forward, this star will be known as Bud's Star, because 'Thomas' is too formal."

Caroline gave Thomas another squeeze, as they continued gazing at the stars. A silent sweet moment shared only by a boy and his mother.

"Why did he leave us?" Thomas said, breaking the silence.

"He hasn't left us." Caroline searched for words. "Your father's research is critical. I'm sure he will be returning any day now."

"But he's been gone over a month, and his note said he

26

would be back soon. Pudge said when his dad left, he didn't come back."

"Thomas, you know your dad is nothing like Pudge's father." Caroline leveled her gaze at her son. "Wherever he is, and whatever he is doing, it is for us."

Thomas looked away. "I know," he whispered.

"Now, let's get ready for bed. Go on. I'll be up in a minute."

Thomas stood to go, then turned to his mother.

"Mom?"

"Yes, dear?"

"I love you."

"I love you, too."

Knowing that Thomas turned and walked back into the house.

———

Thomas slept peacefully in his bed; Caroline watched over him. She bent to kiss her boy. "Sweet dreams, my big, little man."

As she drew back, her foot hit something on the floor, she stopped. What's that? Something was protruding from under Thomas's dresser. She reached and pulled out Thomas's cell phone, the one he had thrown across the room.

She touched the screen, and at one glance, she recognized her husband's text, and her eyes welled up with tears.

Chapter 10

Caroline sat at the kitchen table. Next to her sat a forgotten cup of coffee, long gone cold. Thomas's cell phone sat on the table in front of her. Caroline's face was lit by the blue cast of the message from her husband. She read it one last time. She powered off the phone.

A sharp knock at the door startled Caroline out of her deep thought. *Who could that be at this time of night?* She flipped on the kitchen light, then peeked out the window, recognized the person there. She quickly opened the door.

"Leland!" Caroline exclaimed. "What are you doing here?"

There, in a rumpled wool overcoat, stood Dr. Leland Marcus, one of her husband's senior archaeology colleagues from Edinburgh. He pulled off a stocking cap to reveal a shock of white hair. His face was ruddy and wrinkled like an old paper sack.

"I'm sorry, Caroline," he said in his rich Irish brogue. "I know it is late, but I must talk to you."

"Please come in."

Marcus entered, shrugging off his coat and throwing it

over the back of a chair. He set his leather satchel on the table and surveyed the kitchen. "The boy?" Marcus asked as he rummaged through his bag.

"He's been asleep for a while now. Leland, would you like some tea?"

"No... no."

Caroline could not contain herself any longer. "Leland, what is it?"

Marcus pulled something out of his bag, dropped it with a thud onto the kitchen table. "This!"

It was the charred leather notebook that belonged to Thomas's father.

Chapter 11

Thomas padded down a long dark hallway lined with black, monolithic stones. The sound of breathing was coming from somewhere. Wait a minute. It was coming from him. The hall twisted and turned at weird angles. The walls were closing in on him. He began to run.

The sound of his feet pounded in his ears as it echoed down the nightmare hallway. If he could just run faster, maybe he could get free of the darkness. A turn in the narrowing hall, then another. *What's that?*

A glimmer of light ahead. Almost there. Thomas flew around the corner and found himself bathed in the most glorious sunlight.

Relieved to be out of the eerie hallway, he stood blinking in the brightness, taking in the view. Thomas stood in a green meadow, on the most gorgeous spring day he had ever experienced. His senses were on overload.

The trees, the sky, the waterfall (wow, there was actually a waterfall!) were all in the most vibrant of hues. Thomas was basking in it all when a voice spoke behind him.

"Thomas."

He spun in the direction of the voice.

"Thomas."

There, in the distance, silhouetted in the sun, stood a man. Could it be? He looked so tall and strong. A suitcase sat on the ground next to the man.

Thomas took another step. It was!

"Dad!"

Thomas sprinted to his father, who enveloped him in a huge hug.

"Dad! Oh, Dad! You're home."

Daniel pushed Thomas back from himself, held him by the shoulders.

"Bud, I've still got work to do."

"No. You have to come home."

"I love you, Son," Daniel said with deep sadness.

Thomas's father stood and, picking up his suitcase, turned and moved toward growing dark clouds.

"You have to come home!"

Lightning struck. Daniel didn't flinch but walked steadily on.

"You have to come home! Dad! You have to come home!"

To no avail, Thomas shouted over the raging storm as his father slowly marched away, and finally disappeared into the gray, swirling mist.

"Dad!"

Chapter 12

Thomas bolted upright in his bed. He was covered in sweat.

Still disoriented, he scanned his room. "Dad?" The curtains at the open window whipped in a frenzy. Thunder rumbled in the distance. Thomas hopped out of bed to close the window. And just as he grabbed the sash, lightning crashed startling him. "Mom!"

He dashed down the hall to his parents' bedroom door but didn't enter until he had regained a little of his composure. Then he slowly opened the door and poked his head in. "Mom?"

The room was dark and empty. Then Thomas heard muffled voices drifting up from downstairs. He followed them. It was his mother, and she sounded upset.

"Leland, what are you saying?" Thomas heard her plead.

Thomas followed the voices to the kitchen doorway and silently peered around the doorjamb. Thomas recognized the old disheveled man. He was a fellow professor from the university. Dr. Marcus paced frantically as Caroline sat at the kitchen table. The old man stopped, faced Thomas's mother, and said, "I know where Daniel is."

"What?"

"Well, no, not precisely where he is, but..."

"But what?

Dr. Marcus resumed his pacing, while nervously wringing his wool hat in his hands. "Well, where he left from... or made his exit. No, ah... his leap. Yes, that would be more accurate…"

"Leland, please."

Seeing the pleading in Caroline's eyes, Marcus stopped pacing and nodded. He sat down next to her at the kitchen table.

Caroline reached across the table and took Marcus's hands.

Marcus calmed. "Please forgive me. When Daniel didn't come back that night, I went to Mairead Fhada, searching for some answers. I found his notebook and papers scattered among the stone circle."

"What?"

"I've been going over and over his notes. Which was difficult, because a lot of them are missing. And there was something else strange, Gavin Albright, Daniel's doctoral student, hasn't been seen either."

Caroline's mind was racing.

Marcus tried to reassure her, "I've got someone following up on young Albright."

"But-but, why didn't you tell me this before?" Caroline demanded.

"I didn't want to add to your worry. At least not until I had some answers."

Caroline leaned in. "Do you?"

"I found something. And I admit it sounds far-fetched.

But since none of the other options is possible, the least impossible just might be the answer."

"Well?" Caroline responded, finally losing her patience with the old professor.

"I've been going over Daniel's research, what's left of it. Everything he wrote about Mairead Fhada. It all points in the same direction. You know how Daniel had always seen Mairead Fhada as an ancient place of worship, or an observatory?"

Caroline nodded.

"His most recent notes, from a few days, before he disappeared—uh, before we last saw him—indicate a new piece of research changed his mind about what Mairead Fhada really is."

"What is it?"

Dr. Marcus looked at her gravely. "A door."

Unknown to his mother and Dr. Marcus, Thomas still stood just beyond the room's door, taking in every word. He tried to make sense of it all. Mairead Fhada, a door?

Marcus continued, "According to Daniel's notes, the door is only open a short time... then begins to close... If my calculations are correct, he doesn't have much time to get back."

At this revelation, Thomas's eyes went wide, and he bolted from the house, slamming the door behind him. *I have to get to my dad!* It was all he could think.

"What was that?" exclaimed Dr. Marcus.

Caroline stood with rising concern. "Thomas?"

Chapter 13

Thomas pedaled his bike as fast as he could, straight toward Mairead Fhada's ancient ruins.

Another storm was brewing. Lightning illuminated the sky, and a split-second later, a thunderclap exploded. *That was close.* Thomas raced on

He didn't know what he would do when he reached the ruins. He just knew he had to get there, pulled by the love of his father. Maybe he could figure something out. He had to find his father and bring him home!

Thomas hit a muddy hole and launched from his bike. He hit the ground hard and sprawled exhausted to the ground. He yanked the bike up only to see its front rim twisted out of shape. *Useless!* Lightning flashed again, illuminating the monolithic stones in the distance. He was almost there. "Dad!"

Thomas dropped his ruined bike, and with all the strength he could muster, pushed himself to his feet. As the rain began to fall, he surged on toward his goal, and finally arrived in the circle of monoliths.

"Dad!" Thomas darted among the stones. He searched

round and round the stones until he could search no more. The silent dark stones seem to stare at him defiantly. Finally spent, Thomas leaned his exhausted body against one of the giant pillars. He slid down and collapsed in a heap.

Thomas glared up at the stones now towering over him. They seemed to mock him.

After a beat, he got his breath and moved to get up. Placing his hand on the ground for leverage, he felt something that didn't belong. *What's this?*

He rolled to his knees and separated the tall blades of grass at the base of the stone. He reached between them and pulled out a piece of paper—charred and frayed, wet from the rain, but still legible - His father's diagram of Mairead Fhada.

Chapter 14

Caroline and Dr. Marcus roared across the countryside in Marcus's old Range Rover.

"Leland, why didn't you come sooner?"

The old man frowned in shame. "I had my suspicions... but I—I thought I might just be worrying you needlessly."

———

Thomas studied the charred paper. He immediately recognized the Celtic circle sketched within the perimeter of Mairead Fhada. Glancing from the diagram to the enormous stones, Thomas suddenly understood. He knew what the hand-drawn circle was - a pattern to be followed. If Dr. Marcus said that his dad thought Mairead Fhada was a door, then this must be the combination to unlock the door!

———

Marcus's Range Rover slammed into a pond-sized puddle. The old truck stalled. "Come now! Don't fail me!" Marcus exhorted the Rover. He shut it off, then turned the key again. The engine only groaned. Yet another turn of the key, and this time the engine roared to life.

Marcus threw it into reverse and slammed his foot on the accelerator. The tires just spun in the mud hole. "Come on!"

The old professor tried again. The tires continued spinning.

"I'm truly sorry, lassie. She's stuck fast." Marcus turned toward Caroline. She bolted out of the passenger seat and rushed through the downpour, toward the stone circle of Mairead Fhada and her son.

Chapter 15

Thomas scrambled to his feet and dashed to the center of the ruins. Cross-referencing the diagram and the stones, he rotated the paper, so the graphic was oriented with the actual stones.

That one? Thomas sprinted to the same stone where Daniel had started his strange walk, the twelve-foot high monolith, standing outside the circle, known as Long Meg. Thomas looked around in desperation.

Lightning flashed, and thunder rolled.

Shrack! Kaboom! Lightning struck the stone nearest Thomas, knocking him to the ground. In fear, he dropped the paper and cringed as he slowly squinted up to see the lightning gripping the stone pillar with an electrical hum. He was right!

He grabbed the paper and scurried to his feet. With renewed confidence, he referenced his father's diagram again. Now he knew what to do. He just had to follow the picture.

Thomas walked a loop to the center, then back out to the next stone. Lightning struck that stone and held.

Thomas continued following the drawing's pattern, in what he hoped were his father's footsteps. Stone by illuminated stone, the lightning strikes pushed him on, until he reached the center of the ruins.

Out of breath, he looked up to see every stone clutched by the writhing arms of lightning.

Chapter 16

Caroline stumbled through the wind and the rain. She peered through the storm and saw Mairead Fhada, in the distance, glowing with power.

She could see the terrified Thomas standing at the center of the ruins, surrounded by the glowing, crackling monoliths.

Caroline ran on. She was almost there. She could see her son silhouetted against the white fury. "Thomas!" she called in agony. Over the tempest, Thomas heard his mother's cry. He turned and saw her racing toward him. Across the distance, their eyes met. "Thomas!" she pleaded.

His love for his mother compelled him to stay in this world. His foot inched toward her, then froze. *No.* He commanded himself. *I must find my father. I have to bring him back.* He looked upon his mother one last time.

"Forgive me," he whispered.

Lightning arced from each of the stones, enveloping Thomas and lifting him up. And in a white, blinding flash, he was gone.

Chapter 17

Thomas lay on his back. His pajamas emanated steam. A full moon glowed brightly in the night sky. Stones towered over him, like giant, silent sentries. His eyes twitched. He struggled to sit up, finally succeeded. His hair stood on end.

"Whoa!" exclaimed Thomas. Staggering to his feet, he could hardly walk a straight line. And whatever Mairead Fhada he had started out in, this was clearly not the same place… or perhaps not the same time?

While the standing stones looked familiar, Thomas realized there were more of them—standing, that is. Basically, the same site, but it seemed not-so-ancient somehow. Then it hit him.

There were no toppled stones here. This is what Mairead Fhada must have looked like in its original construction.

Thomas peered between the stones, and his breath fled away. The moon cast eerie shadows everywhere, and where he should have seen the distant lights of the village, he saw only a dark, unspoiled forest.

Thomas strained his eyes, searching that distance for any sign of life or light. But only a breeze rippled through those trees, making them sway in a giant rhythmic dance. A shiver ran through his body.

With growing foreboding, Thomas sensed he was not alone. He whirled around and encountered… no one. He strained his adjusting eyes harder, and mustered up enough courage to shout. But his voice came out as just a tiny squeak: "Who's out there?"

Still nothing. But Thomas couldn't shake the feeling he was being watched by someone at the dark forest's edge. The full moon, high and bright, pushed that forest's shadows nearer to Thomas.

In the blue twilight, it was almost imperceptible where the actual forest stopped, and the shadows began.

And then he saw it—movement at the nearest edge of the tallest tree's longest shadow. He first thought it might only be the wind blowing the trees harder. But then he heard a low, faint, rustling, scratching… like the wind, but somehow different.

Unable to stop himself, Thomas took a few steps toward the forest's edge. There, the sound seemed to emanate from the longest of the shadows. What was that?

Then, unbelievably, before Thomas could even fathom it, the shadow of that tallest tree began to expand toward him, gathering speed and breadth as it skittered across the ground. Thomas's mind reeled, unable to comprehend what he saw.

The scratching sound grew as the shadow continued to stretch and writhe toward him. Slowly, the shadow's leading-edge separated itself from the ground, and rose to become a large, human-looking hand, but gloved in black.

Thomas stood frozen. The black-gloved hand reached for Thomas, even as Thomas watched, in horror, as the moving hand grew an arm, then a torso, then the entire ghastly figure of a heavily armed medieval warrior all in black.

Nearly six-and-a-half-feet tall, the shadow warrior towered over Thomas, and its long dark cloak rustled in the cold breeze.

Its face was hidden by a metal helm with only slits for seeing. The helm of the dark warrior turned toward Thomas, and the eyes there glowed red and hot like lava. Those burning eyes told Thomas, whatever soul this being might have had, was undoubtedly now long gone.

Thomas turned to run but was paralyzed as he saw a host of other shadow warriors morphing out of the darkness all around him. He opened his mouth to scream. But no sound came as the shadows engulfed him.

Chapter 18

A dark, horse-drawn, jailer's wagon raced through the forest, pulled by powerful black horses whose hooves pounded the earth, and whose eyes rolled in fury as hot exhalations shot from their nostrils in steam.

Two hulking shadow warriors drove the box-like paddy wagon; one of them cracked a long whip over the horses, and they galloped faster still.

Inside the rough-walled box, Thomas sat quivering in a corner, gripped with fear. He chanced a look out the barred window.

The forest flew by; it was blanketed in a thick fog that the moonlight just barely showed through. *I have to get out of here!* Thomas thought in a panic. His eyes fell on the rustic metal latch on the coach's door.

He grabbed and twisted at it as hard as he could, but to no avail. It was stuck fast, probably locked from the outside.

So Thomas grabbed the window bars and pulled with all his might, then pushed. Strain and desperation made sweat spring from his forehead and roll into his eyes. But the bars stayed immovable.

He pressed his face to the bars, straining to see anything outside that might help him. He could just make out the moon above the dark horizon. For a moment, there was a break in the forest, and the wheels clattered over a wooden bridge. Thomas could hear a rushing river below them. "Help!" he cried. "Someone, please help me!"

Suddenly the moon was eclipsed for a split second, as something huge passed over the wagon with a rush of wind. The horses squealed in terror, and the carriage lurched to an abrupt stop. Thomas was thrown to the iron-covered floor.

A clamor arose from outside. Some huge beast growled, and clashes of steel rang through the air. Thomas peered out the window again, but the fog obscured everything.

As the sword clashes continued, Thomas abruptly tried the door handle again. This time it turned, with a slow screech of rusted metal. As quietly as possible, he slowly opened the door, crept out onto a little step, then eased himself to the ground.

He stood a moment, shivering and vulnerable, as the sounds of an unseeable battle surrounded him. He strained to see through the fog, but could only make out vague, fast-moving shapes. *This is my chance*, he thought. *I am out of here!*

He broke into a wild sprint. In the thick fog, a big shadow suddenly blocked his way. Thomas darted in another direction and sought refuge behind a large tree that he had nearly run into. He spun with his back to the tree, his eyes darting to and fro. Trying to hold his breath, he listened intently, orienting himself to where the mist-shrouded battle was taking place.

There were more growls, clangs of iron, cries of

pain… then silence. In the silence, Thomas stood petrified, unsure of what to do or which way to go. He finally decided: *I'm heading away from this craziness, as far into the forest as I can go.*

He turned to run and plowed right into a towering dark figure. He gasped, looked up, and, as he realized he was caught again. His eyes rolled back in his head and he fainted.

Chapter 19

Total darkness. Thomas wondered if he was blind, or worse yet, dead. He waved his hand in front of his face, perceived that his eyes were slowly adjusting to the dark.

Now he saw there was a faint, moving, crack of light above him. He groped and pushed against his containment, then realized he must be inside a large bag of some sort. It smelled of leather and earth.

He squirmed in his cramped quarters, then stopped. Something was pushing against the side of the bag. Slowly in… slowly out… in… out... Thomas put his ear against the grainy leather and held his breath.

He listened and heard the unmistakable sound of deep breathing. And then —a rhythm like large wings beating the wind. And over the sounds came the voices of two normal-sounding men with British-sounding accents, except not modern.

"We should have waited," the first voice said.

The second man responded, "John, we knew the risks."

"I'm sick of this war," the John fellow said with disgust. "Who is going to tell his family?"

"It's your turn." The second man responded with finality.

"Fine. I'll meet you back at the stronghold."

"Be careful, my friend."

"For the kingdom."

"For the kingdom!" the other responded.

There was another rush of wind, and the wing-flapping sound separated into two sets of wing-flapping sounds, in different rhythms, with one of them becoming faint, then gone.

Curiosity drove Thomas to grope about the bag, and, finally, he was able to find a tie at the top. He managed to loose it and, pushing back the flap, he peeked out.

What he saw took his breath from him.

It was still night. The tops of trees were dropping away. Fear came because Thomas was never one to love heights. But curiosity was stronger, so Thomas pushed the flap higher and raised his head out for a better look.

His hands clenched tightly to the big bag's lip. The wind caught his hair. He could hardly believe what he was seeing.

He was hundreds of feet in the air. The leather bag that held him, he now realized, was a large saddlebag. And the saddlebag was secured to the massive back of a flying dragon!

Chapter 20

The dragon was a magnificent beast, golden-brown in color, with a smooth-scaled leathery hide. And at full extension, its mighty wings comfortably stretched out at least forty feet.

Thomas couldn't believe it. "I'm riding in a saddlebag thrown over the back of a giant flying lizard!" he whispered to himself.

The view was incredible: starry sky, full moon, crystal lakes sparkling in the moonlight, and approaching majestic mountains capped with snow. He was flying!

His wonder and awe overcame his vertigo and fear. All the while, he heard the beating of the magnificent beast's powerful wings. Suddenly the world glowed white. They were inside a cloud, then out. For now, Thomas forgot all his troubles. He was flying on the back of a dragon!

"So, he lives."

Thomas, startled from his exhilaration, shrank back into the bag.

Hearty laughter, "Breathe, lad—I'm one of the good fellows!"

Encouraged by the voice's warmth and laughter, Thomas cautiously peeked out of the bag again.

Atop the dragon, straddling a saddle cinched around its belly, sat a man—in his late thirties, Thomas reckoned.

He looked solidly rugged and strong-muscled as if he'd seen much training and many battles. To Thomas, he seemed to exude danger and adventure.

But the man's feature that struck Thomas most were his piercing gray eyes—the color of a storm. Gazing at this man, Thomas had the strangest thought: *Even though I'm just a kid, if this guy asked me, I think I'd follow him right into a battle.*

Finding his voice, Thomas asked, "Where are you taking me?"

"Someplace safe," replied the man.

"Away from those dark guys?" Thomas asked, hopefully.

The man looked at Thomas with fatherly concern.

"Yes," he said reassuringly. "Yes, away from the dark ones."

Thomas smiled with relief.

"Climb on up here, boy; you'll get a better view. And I'm sure it's more comfortable than riding in that saddle-bag. Just heft yourself using the bag strap."

Thomas hesitated a moment, then carefully climbed out of the bag and up the strap, just like the man suggested.

But Thomas's move from the saddlebag to the back of the man's saddle was un-anchored, and Thomas lost his balance. His eyes widened as the fall loomed, but the man quickly caught Thomas's arm and swung him back up onto the saddle.

"Hold on."

"Thanks!" Thomas wrapped his arms firmly around the man's waist.

"I am known as Deacon," the man said over his shoulder. "And this," he said, slapping the great dragon's shoulder, "is Thorn."

The dragon trumpeted in response then turned his huge triangular head toward them in greeting; his luminous golden eyes twinkled.

"What do they call you?" asked Deacon.

"They call me... uh, my name is Thomas."

"Well, Thomas, are you holding on?"

"Yes?"

"Tighter," commanded Deacon.

And with that, the great dragon dipped his head and went into a steep dive, with Thomas holding onto the man for dear life. The boy would've screamed, but the rushing air sucked the wind right out of his lungs.

Deacon made a small chuk-chuk noise, and the dragon leveled off. Deacon pointed to a dark shadow above them. Thomas could barely make it out. Deacon said: "Shadow warrior."

"What?" asked Thomas.

Deacon ignored Thomas's question because he was quickly scanning the approaching cliffs. His eyes latched on a rocky outcropping. He leaned down and pointed over the dragon's right side.

"There, Thorn. Get us in there."

Diving and angling at the same time, Thorn effortlessly glided to a soft landing on the side of a cliff behind the rock outcropping; the moon's gleam kept them in shadow. The dragon's sharp talons gripped a craggy boulder, holding them steady.

Thorn and Deacon sat silently, and the only sound came from the giant dragon's heavy breathing. Thomas looked around. When he could no longer stand it, he broke the silence with: "Excuse me, sir..."

Immediately Deacon twisted and clamped his hand over Thomas's mouth; with fierce eyes, Deacon put his index finger to his lips.

Thomas got the picture, but Deacon's hand didn't release him.

Suddenly a huge shadow passed over them. Thomas looked up, and his eyes grew wide with fear. About eighty feet overhead, flying in front of the stars, was the shadow warrior, on a bigger black beast. This dragon's sinewy black body was covered in light-sucking scales. Thomas remembered why he didn't like snakes.

He looked at Deacon, seeking reassurance. Deacon shook his head, communicating it still was not okay to make noise. Even Thorn held his breath

The shadow passed, then another ten seconds; Deacon searched the sky the entire time. Finally, he sighed out his breath and released Thomas.

"Sorry about that, boy. Shadow warrior scouts make me nervous, and that one was close."

Thorn growled petulantly.

"You don't have to tell me that was close. You weigh a ton, and think you know everything."

Thorn rumbled again, for emphasis, and Deacon gave Thomas a knowing smirk and rolled his eyes; the man and the dragon knew each other well. His calm returned, Deacon nudged Thorn with the heel of his boot and commanded: "Let's give that shadow warrior and his beast a wide berth. Up, Thorn!"

And with that, the mighty beast leaped into the sky and soared on.

Chapter 21

The heels of six heavy boots striking the stone floor echoed down the hallway and bounced off the large rough-hewn doors at the end. The seven-foot-tall General Nawg, commander of the shadow warriors, marched several paces in front of two shorter-but-bulkier shadow warriors. They maintained that distance carefully, because of their fear of the general.

All shadow-warrior troops knew that getting too close to their general was to risk annihilation—those that didn't know this were already gone.

And while the hallway was lit by torches, Nawg's dark cloak and countenance sucked in whatever dim light those torches cast. Only his battle-scarred iron breastplate reflected a faint glow.

The two warriors behind Nawg dragged a beaten and bruised man. From his leather jacket it was clear that he was a Dragon Rider. The cortege halted at the massive doors. The man's injured head lolled back and forth in semi-consciousness.

General Nawg shoved the heavy doors open like they

were made of balsa, then stepped into a cavernous hall and dropped the prisoner to the floor, where his swollen eye slits barely opened. Having deposited the prisoner they came to attention. Then, incredibly, the colossal general and his warriors kneeled.

"My lord," General Nawg hissed, as he bent his helm toward the stone floor.

Across the dim hall, silhouetted by a roaring blaze from a large fireplace, stood an even-darker figure. He slowly turned to his loyal general, whose head was still bowed in obeisance.

Lord Darcon, ruler of the dark lands, looked upon the loyal leader of his shadow army, who raised his head and turned his helm toward his master. His eye slits glowed red. And while Darcon was not quite six feet all, the much-taller general actually shuddered, almost imperceptibly, when Darcon's cold, gray steel gaze pierced him. The other soldiers felt it too.

"What is this?" demanded the dark lord.

"My master," responded Nawg, "Our troops were ambushed... the new Otherlander was taken. We captured this rebel, and I brought him to you after interrogating him."

Darcon approached and examined the prone man. Darcon bent, reached out, and almost-tenderly patted the man's face... then roughly grabbed a tuft of hair and jerked the man's face up to his own.

The pain broke the prisoner's semi consciousness; he blanched and recoiled as he realized whose breath was washing over him.

"Where is the Otherlander?" Darcon demanded. "You certainly know—the traveler who recently came through the door?"

The prisoner shook his head violently, getting free of

Darcon's grip. And a fire deep within the man glinted through his swollen eyes. Scrambling and back-pedaling, the man managed to get to his feet.

Standing defiantly, he whispered through his cracked lips, "For the kingdom!" even as the two shadow warriors grabbed his arms and forced him to his knees.

Darcon's face distorted. *How could this one endure Nawg's tortures and still stand with this confidence? Doesn't he know who he is facing? Doesn't he understand he is facing his immediate demise?!*

Seething rage and hatred now mushroomed within Darcon. He swiftly reached within his robe, extracted a wicked dagger, and in two steps plunged it into the man's chest. Then he twisted it.

The prisoner groaned, then crumpled to the floor. His life left him in one final defiant breath: "For the kingdom..."

Darcon was shaken for a moment, and then quickly regained his composure. He bellowed: "Find the new Otherlander and bring him to me, or you will die more painfully than this one!"

Chapter 22

"Do you live here?" Thomas asked as Thorn, and his riders landed on the outskirts of a small stone-and-thatch peasant village. Deacon dismounted, then helped Thomas slide down from the saddle as he said: "No. I have some business to attend to here, and then we're off again."

After leaving Thorn in a stable hewn out of a nearby cliff's face, Deacon and Thomas walked into the village. As they made their way, it became apparent that Thomas, still dressed in his 21st-century graphic t-shirt, sweatpants, and walking barefoot, was drawing attention.

"We've got to get you some real clothes," Deacon said, frowning down at the disheveled boy. "What were you doing in Darcon's territory? Especially half-dressed?"

"I was looking for my dad," Thomas answered as he averted his gaze from another gawking villager.

"What?"

"We got separated."

Deacon guided Thomas into a merchant's shop. It reminded Thomas of an old General store Thomas liked to visit with his Grandfather in his small hometown in

Northern California. Wooden shelves to the ceiling stacked neatly with supplies of all sorts, kegs filling the floor full of who knows what and the sweet smell of tobacco and leather filled the air.

"How?" Deacon asked as he rummaged through a small stack of tunics on one wall.

The merchant-tradesman approached, surveying Thomas quizzically.

"Your boy needs some garments?"

"How could you tell?"

"Tunic and some trousers?" the tradesman responded eagerly.

Deacon looked Thomas up and down; he was not impressed by what he saw. He focused on the bare feet. Shaking his head, he sighed: "Better add some boots as well."

The man smiled at the prospect and immediately selected likely items to check against Thomas for size. All the while, he muttered a little song to himself.

Deacon turned back to Thomas. "How did you lose him?"

"Huh?"

"You said you lost your father. How did you lose him?"

Thomas stopped as a flood of memories broke over his mind. His father, his mother, the great times, moving to England, all the excitement of his father's research.

He could hardly force himself to think it, much less say it. "Oh... well, my dad... he's a professor, and we came to England so he could do some research... and then he went on a trip, and he..."

Thomas couldn't get the words out. He hated it when he got this lump in his throat. His eyes began to burn, but he determined he would not cry.

Deacon understood only enough of Thomas's words to mercifully finish the boy's thought, "He never came back?"

To hear someone else say out loud what he was thinking inside made him angry. They didn't have the right!

"No," Thomas said forcefully. "He is coming back! And I'm here to find him!"

"I see."

Thomas tried to think of more to say about that, but the tradesman returned with a stack of goods.

"Will there be anything else?"

"Aye," responded Deacon. "Throw in some tickle juice for the lad."

"Tickle juice?" Thomas asked.

"Yeah, it's a drink children here enjoy," Deacon said as he paid the man for the goods.

The clerk plopped the tunic, trousers, and boots—as well as a small bottle of juice with a cork capping it—into Thomas's unsuspecting arms. Deacon turned to head for the door.

"You stay here and change," Deacon said, as he headed out the door. "I've got to take care of that business."

Chapter 23

Thomas stood in the general store. He surveyed the shop, looking for a place to change out of his pajamas. *Great! I'm alone again.* Then he felt someone staring at him.

He turned and saw a sharp-nosed, beady-eyed little man watching him. As their eyes met, the man quickly set off in a strange twitchy motion that reminded Thomas of a weasel. Thomas got a hold of his pile of clothes and stumbled for the door after Deacon.

"Hey, wait! I think I'll go with you!"

Thomas scurried up the dirt road and caught up with Deacon.

"Sir," said Thomas, still trying to manage the clothes and the bottle of juice while also keeping pace with Deacon's long strides.

"I'm sure my dad is here. Can you help me find him?"

"Darcon has filled this land with orphans."

"Sir, I'm not an orphan!"

"Look, he's not with me… and this isn't the best time to be nosing around. When we get out of this territory we can talk about your missing father."

They reached the entrance to a tavern. Deacon placed his heavy hand on Thomas's shoulder.

"I'll only be a moment. No children allowed, so drink your juice and do your best not to draw attention to yourself."

Deacon pushed open the rough tavern door and went in. Thomas peered up and down the street, then noticed an alley to one side of the tavern.

Thomas hurried to carry all his new stuff about halfway down the alley, set the juice bottle on a wooden keg there, then quickly hid behind the cask and changed into his new trousers. He put the juice bottle in one of the pockets. He brushed the dust off his feet and pulled on the new leather boots admiring their patina. Then, just as he was putting on his new tunic, he noticed a window in the wall above the keg.

Thomas scrambled atop the keg and, peering through the window into the tavern, saw Deacon talking to the man behind the bar.

The man pointed to a door further back in the room. A young girl passed a mug to Deacon. Deacon took his ale and headed to the back, then knocked quietly on that door. The door cracked open a fraction. He exchanged hurried words, then entered and closed the door behind him.

Thomas turned away. *What was that all about?* He slid down the wall, plopping to a seat atop the keg. His legs dangled far above the ground. Then he remembered the juice. He pulled the little bottle from his pocket, looked at it quizzically, then pulled the cork from the bottle's mouth.

"Here goes nothin'."

Thomas took a sip. His eyes squinted, and his face distorted, then his eyes opened, and a huge smile spread across his face. "Wow! Not bad!" he exclaimed, and took another swig as the alley door opened and a hooded person stepped out. They looked down the alley, then quickly turned and bumped into Thomas. Thomas got a peek under the hood and saw that it was the girl from inside the tavern. She adjusted her hood down, hiding her face, and scurried out of the alley.

Thomas watched her go and disappear into the peopled streets. He surveyed the town.

The buildings were all made of stone. People and livestock roamed up and down the dirt streets. Here and there, vendors hawked their wares.

Across the way, something caught Thomas's eye. *Who is that? There! And there he is again!*

Thomas finally made out, behind one of the street vendors, that weasel-looking man from the store. Not good. That guy must have followed them. Thomas looked up and down the street. *What should I do?*

He glanced back to where the weasel-man had been standing. Gone! Then Thomas saw the man talking to someone around the corner of a building. *Who was he talking to?*

It was the girl from the tavern. Still hooded she had a quick word then just as quickly surreptitiously exchanged something with the Weasel. Then she blended into the crowd and was gone.

Then, to Thomas's horror, three dark-robed giants stepped around the corner—shadow warriors! Thomas stood, frozen in fear and indecision, as things switched to slow motion, and the Weasel pointed right at him. His blood chilled as the warriors turned their helm covered heads and locked their burning red gazes on him.

Chapter 24

Move, Thomas—move! The boy tried to motivate his frozen body. "I said, Move!"

And with that, he was off. He ran into the alley next to the pub, scrambling for a place to hide. He spied a door in the back of the building! He ran to it and pounded his small fist as hard as he could.

"Who is it?" a deep voice demanded from behind the closed door.

"It's me. Thomas! And, uh, uh…" *What was that guy's name?* Oh yeah! "Deacon. I have to speak to Deacon!"

The door opened a crack. An arm poked through and jerked Thomas through the opening.

"What are you doing, yelling my name to the world like that?" Deacon demanded. "Do you know what secret means?"

"A strange man was watching me and then... he, uh..." Thomas stammered.

"Spit it out!"

Thomas took a deep breath and shouted: "Shadow warriors!"

Deacon's frustration turned to focus. He addressed the man.

"We must be off!"

He shook the man's hand. "For the kingdom."

"For the kingdom!"

Deacon and Thomas slipped out the back door and snuck up the alley. Out of habit, Deacon reached back to take Thomas's hand. Thomas stared at the man's outstretched hand a moment, then accepted his grip.

Deacon's hand completely enveloped Thomas's; the strength and the coarseness of the calluses from years of dragon's reins gave reassurance to the boy. They came to the edge of the alley, carefully peered around the corner. The shadow warriors were talking to "the Weasel," as Thomas designated him.

"Maybe he didn't see me," Thomas offered hopefully.

That hope died instantly. The Weasel pointed right at them, then at the tavern's rear door. Two of the shadow warriors marched purposefully in their direction, and the other headed down another alley.

"Uh-oh," Thomas groaned.

"Run!" Deacon urgently whispered. And he was off. Thomas was frozen a moment, then took off after Deacon as fast as his legs could carry him.

"Wait for me!"

Deacon stopped to allow Thomas to catch up, then scooped him up and threw him over his shoulder like a sack of potatoes. The man bolted on down the narrow alley.

Thomas looked up from his backward position over Deacon's shoulder, to see the shadow warriors closing in.

"Run faster! Must run faster!" urged Thomas.

Deacon put his fingers to his lips and let out a shrill whistle.

Though nearly two streets away, the stabled Thorn heard his master's summons and raised his head from consuming a massive piece of venison, bits of it still dangling from his mouth. Thorn grunted, then bowed to continue his tasty meal.

Deacon had put a little distance between himself and the dark soldiers.

"Thorn!" he yelled.

Thorn lifted his head again, moaned, and returned to his meal. He wasn't ready to pull himself away from his savory, long-awaited supper.

Deacon and Thomas rounded a tree.

"Thorn!!!" Deacon shouted at the top of his lungs as he got within yards of the stable's entrance and Thorn.

The great dragon rose to attention. Deacon ran up, swung Thomas into Thorn's saddle, and turned just in time to duck the swinging metal orb of the first shadow warrior's mace.

Deacon had his sword instantly out and swinging, but the mace-wielding shadow warrior backed out of its range. The two combatants crossed mace chain with sword blade, and there was lots of ducking on both sides. Deacon intentionally tried to draw the shadow warrior away from Thomas and Thorn.

But Deacon didn't realize that the second dark soldier had gone to Thorn's other side, and was whispering to Thomas while stealthily pulling his sword: "Boy!" Reflexively, Thomas turned in response.

"Come to me, boy," the warrior hissed through his helm, and the bloodless, wraithlike voice froze Thomas. He could only watch, wide-eyed in fear, as the warrior's gloved hand reached to snatch him.

"Hh-e-l-pp!" Thomas barely croaked out as the shadow warrior's hand came closer. And that's when

Thorn's mighty muscled tail slammed into the second warrior, sending him arcing through the air until he smashed into a boulder. He rolled off the stone, a broken heap.

Thomas snapped out of his paralysis. "Wow, Thorn!" he said in awe. "Home run!" And he petted the dragon like a big dog. "Good dragon!"

Thorn snorted in response, then realized his master was pinned against a fence, with the mace-swinger blocking his sword parries and wearing him down.

Thorn rose to move where he could use his tail again, and Thomas grabbed at the saddle horn reflexively—while also enjoying the feeling of all this power under him.

But that enjoyment was short-lived, as there was a rush of wind, and a dark shadow passed over, momentarily obscuring the sun. Thomas looked up, but before he could react, he heard a terrible screech, and massive talons plucked him off of Thorn's saddle and high into the air.

Chapter 25

Thomas screamed as the ground fell away at a dizzying rate. He was being lifted higher and higher in the clutches of the third shadow warrior's flying beast. The monster's black hide glinted in the sunlight, and its eyes smoldered like fiery coals.

Thomas kicked and yelled, but to no avail. There was no breaking the vise-like grip. Looking down, Thomas weighed his options: Be eaten by a black dragon monster? Or fall from this height?

One more look at the giant, disgusting, bat-like lizard and Thomas continued his struggle. *I'll take my chances,* Thomas thought.

The beast sensed the struggle, turned his angular head toward Thomas, and emitted a blood-curdling screech. Thomas tried to cover his ears from the piercing blast.

Back on the ground, Deacon blocked another mace swing and parried feverishly—to keep the mace-swinger unaware of Thorn's gradual movements behind him.

And at just the right time, Thorn's tail tapped the shadow warrior on the butt, he looked surprised, and that was more than enough time for Deacon to slice his blade rapidly upward, expertly slicing just a fraction under the shadow warrior's metal helm.

The warrior's head went tumbling end-over-end. His body hung for a minute, then toppled lifelessly to the dirt.

Deacon leaped back onto Thorn's saddle.

"Up, Thorn!"

With Thorn's booming battle cry, they were after Thomas, rocketing into the sky.

The mighty beating of Thorn's powerful wings quickly closed the distance to the ebony beast and his rider.

Thorn trumpeted.

Still dangling from the beast's iron talons, Thomas looked back. Hearing the call of his newfound giant friend, he suddenly went from despair to hope.

"Thorn!"

The shadow warrior and his mount wheeled to meet the attack.

Thomas watched helplessly as Thorn and Deacon bore down on his position.

"Oh please, oh please, oh please—God help me!"

The beasts and riders hurtled toward each other; Deacon and the shadow warrior both pulled their swords, like medieval jousters in the sky.

Seeing Thorn hurtling toward it, the shadow warrior's beast dropped Thomas from his clutches.

Thomas screamed as he fell.

Deacon saw the boy plummeting. "Thomas!" Then: "Thorn, get him."

Thorn trumpeted his agreement, and they swooped under the approaching black beast and dove toward Thomas.

Seeing the ground's swift approach, Thomas continued screaming.

Deacon bent in the saddle. Dragon and rider torpedoed toward the helpless boy—focused, muscles taut, ready to spring. As their trajectories met, Deacon snatched Thomas from mid-air and swung him back into the safety of the saddle behind him.

Thomas clung to Deacon. "That was close," he gasped, overcome with relief. Deacon looked at the ground, measuring the distance in his mind. He said sardonically, "Oh, you were still at least two dragon-lengths from the ground." *That doesn't sound all that far to me!* Thomas thought.

Thorn landed. Deacon helped Thomas slide to the ground.

But Thomas didn't immediately release his grip on Deacon's hand. Catching Deacon's eye, the boy said heartily: "Thank you."

Deacon softened a bit.

"Stay here, lad, and out of sight. I'll be right back." Then: "Up, Thorn."

Thomas watched with awe as his rescuers launched back into the sky.

"Go get 'em!" Thomas whispered as he watched the dragon and his rider climb to meet the shadow warrior and his beast.

The shadow warrior noticed his followers. Reining his dragon into a tight turn, he spurred his beast to meet the challengers. Thorn beat his mighty wings, picking up speed. Beat-for-beat, the black monster matched Thorn's pace, and the two careened toward each other.

Deacon cringed, bracing for impact, "This will hurt."

Whoomp! The dragons collided in mid-air, becoming a tangle of wings, talons, and teeth. The beasts clung to each other, clawing and biting while their riders hung on tight and tried to stab each other in passing.

Each dragon gripped one of the other dragon's wings with jagged teeth, so they were no longer flying, they spun toward the ground. Realizing this, both Deacon and the shadow warrior tried to stab at the head of his opponent's dragon to make it release the hampered wing.

Then Deacon snuck a glance at the fast-approaching ground and yelled: "Thorn!"

Thorn refused to release his enemy. "Thorn!!"

Thorn ignored him, and the ground loomed ever closer. Resigned to his death, Deacon stabbed at the black dragon's head again and put out one of its eyes.

Bellowing in pain, it released Thorn's wing, and, at the last possible moment, Thorn flapped and maneuvered to be above the black beast. The beast was now falling upside down, with the shadow warrior still strapped in the saddle under him.

Deacon, realizing, screamed: "Now, Thorn!!!"

Thorn pushed off the other dragon's chest and launched back into the sky.

The upside-down shadow warrior stopped trying to get himself unstrapped, and entirely took in the granite surface that would end him. His body began to blur and turn to shadow, but there wasn't enough time to morph!

He screamed as Deacon muttered: "Go back to the one who spawned you." The dark beast slammed into the ground, and the crushed shadow warrior went silent.

Thorn looked one last time on his enemy, then turned and gave a mighty roar of victory.

Deacon reined his dragon. "Come on, Thorn. Let's go get the boy."

Chapter 26

"Not bad, eh?" remarked Deacon, as his teeth tugged another bite of meat off the charred skewer in his hand.

Thomas and Deacon sat eating in a large cave, huddled close to a small campfire. The fire's flickering light cast shadows on the cave's rock walls and ceiling. Thorn lay near them. His giant body formed a backrest for Deacon, and his tail was wrapped protectively near Thomas.

"Boy, I guess I was pretty hungry," remarked Thomas. He wiped his mouth on his sleeve. "What is this?"

"Cliff rat."

Thomas let that sink in. "Hmm. I know it's a total cliche but— it tastes like chicken."

The campfire crackled. Deacon stared into its flames, content with the silence.

"So, where we headed now?" Thomas asked.

"Home."

"Is it far?"

"Yes, another day or so as the dragon flies."

Thomas pondered this a moment. "You're a long way from home. I bet your family can't wait to see you."

Deacon continued staring into the flames.

"You know—a wife, some kids?"

"I don't have a family," Deacon responded flatly. "Too busy fighting shadow warriors."

Thomas decided to change the subject.

"Who are they? The shadow warriors, I mean."

"Darcon's henchmen."

"Are they after you?"

"Let's just say, I'm a pretty popular guy," Deacon smirked.

"Why is that?"

"I have something Darcon wants?"

"What's that?"

"My head."

Thomas took that in, then asked: "What's going on here? How'd this all start?"

Chapter 27

Deacon finished his last bite, then threw that skewer in the fire and took a swig from his leather canteen. After wiping his mouth, he leaned in. The campfire cast an eerie glow on his face as he said:

"Nalbion was once a peaceful and flourishing kingdom. The royal family was kind and benevolent to their subjects. Then, many years ago, a traveler with vast knowledge came to the castle to tutor the prince.

"This tutor quickly gained favor with the king. The tutor soon became a royal advisor—and, at the same time, grew in power beyond the palace. Unbeknownst to the king, the advisor was forming an alliance with a band of evil priests known as the Shadow Cult.

"With these priests, the advisor began to practice all forms of evil magic, to do what ought not to be done. Using their dark magic, they opened the door to the Shadow Realm and made an alliance with the dark ones— the deformed men and dragons who are the shadow warriors and their hideous beasts."

Thomas listened intently, the darkness outside the cave

seemed to creep into his soul. He couldn't help but scoot a little closer to the fire.

Deacon continued: "And on one frightful night, the advisor and his followers… murdered the royal family. And that man's name was Darcon."

Thomas leaned forward.

"Darcon and those loyal to him quickly subdued and oppressed the subjects of Nalbion, slaying thousands in the process. Still, there is a small band of men and women who, though forced into hiding, oppose him with their lives, and plot to overthrow him. We will restore Nalbion to the place it once was."

Finished with the story, Deacon leaned back against Thorn. But Thomas wasn't satisfied: "Wait. So these dark guys, the shadow warriors, they're shadows, right? So how can you kill a shadow?"

An owl hooted somewhere in the night. Thomas flinched.

"Shadow warriors have to materialize to do anything in the physical world, like hold a sword or strike one of us. When they are in their physical form, they can be killed just like you or I… so long as they are no more than three moments into their shadow-turn."

Thomas sat back, thinking it through.

"That's how the one who fell was killed."

"Aye, he didn't have time to turn back to shadow." Deacon winked.

A low rumble rolled through the cave, and a stench arose from Thorn's rear end.

"Thorn!" Thomas grimaced and ran out of the cave, waving his hand in front of his nose. "That's horrible!" the boy uttered between grimacing breaths.

"That's it. No more cliff-rat for you, beast." Deacon's voice echoed out of the cave.

Thorn whimpered.

Thomas suddenly got a glint in his eye and ran back into the cave. He sat next to Deacon and leaned in toward the fire with a mischievous grin.

"Okay, I've got a story for you."

Taking a deep breath, Thomas began with his best scary voice: "It happened on a dark and stormy night. A young couple was parking and listening to the radio.

"Suddenly the news came on, and an announcer said: 'Warning! An insane murderer has just escaped from the local asylum. Beware, he is considered extremely danger-ous. He is six feet tall with dark hair, and in place of his right hand there is'"—Thomas whipped up his hand with one finger curled—"'a hook!'"

Deacon yawned.

"Get it? A hook!" Thomas waved his crooked finger in the air.

"Enough stories," Deacon said, standing and retrieved a blanket from Thorn's saddlebag. "Time to sleep. We have a long day tomorrow, and we need to be at our best."

Thorn growled.

"I know!" Deacon slapped Thorn's haunches. "You are always at your best."

Deacon threw the blanket to Thomas. Then tossed another log on the fire, plopped on the ground, rolled over with his back to the heat, and settled in for the night.

Thomas, unsure of himself, laid down and tried to get comfortable. He closed his eyes, then, suddenly, sat up, searching the ground, he found a large rock and tossed it out of the mouth of the cave. Satisfied that the earth was as comfortable as he could make it, he laid back down again, stared at the ceiling of the cave and watched the shadows flicker.

"Deacon? Are you asleep?"

"Yes," came the gruff response.

"Oh."

Silence.

"Deacon?"

"What?

"Are we going to find my dad?"

Silence.

"Deacon?"

"I don't know?"

Thomas sat up. "Seriously, you don't know?" He said to Deacon's back.

"I don't want to get your hopes up. Now, go to sleep," responded the rider without budging.

Thomas stared at the back of the rider then finally laid back down.

Deacon, wrapped in his blanket, could hear Thomas muttering to himself. Hearing the boy asking for his father, the dragon rider couldn't help but relive the past. All the fighting, all the pain, the loss. He willed the memories away, pushing them deep down and drifted off into a fitful sleep.

Thomas gritted his teeth in anger, laying under his rough blanket. *What a jerk*, he thought. *I have to find my dad. Until I find him, I can't go home.* He wondered what his mom was doing right now. *I'll find him. No matter what.* His eyes were heavy, and exhaustion soon won, and Thomas slipped off into a dream. He was being chased by a dark shadow through a strange land, and he was all alone.

Chapter 28

Thomas's eyes popped open. Had he heard something? He was cold. The fire now was only a smolder. He sat up quietly and looked over at Deacon who hadn't moved. The dragon, Thorn was also sleeping. Thomas could see the rhythmic pumping of his sides as he breathed deeply. Thomas fumed about Deacon's treatment of him before they went to sleep. As he sat up quietly and wrapped his blanket about himself he hatched a plan. Thomas would go after his dad himself. If he had really stopped to think about it, he would have known he was lying to himself. He was self-deceived but that is the way of anger. He was blinded to the reality around him. *I'll show him*, Thomas thought as he quickly grabbed a canteen of water and fastening his jacket, slipped out of the cave, and into the darkness.

Chapter 29

It took Thomas quite a while to make it down the side of the cliff. A couple of times, he found himself in a precarious position and considered climbing back up, but he continued on fueled by his anger at Deacon and his desire to find his father.

Now he found himself at the foot of the cliff considering the dense forest that lay before him. He peered back over his shoulder, where he could see the dark hole of the cave halfway up the cliff. Deacon and Thorn were probably still sleeping. He turned back to the forest and stepped in among the giant trees.

He quickly found a trail and begin following it. This wasn't so bad after all. No sooner had he felt his confidence rising when somewhere in the distance an animal howled. A wolf? *Do they have wolves in this world?* He stopped, frozen in his tracks. Maybe he was hearing things. Then, another howl answered the first, and then a third. They were getting closer. Thomas turned, cursing his stupidity, and begin making his way back toward the base of the cliff.

The break in the forest was just ahead. A low growl

rumbled somewhere close behind him. He glanced over his shoulder and saw the glint of red eyes through the brush then took off in a full sprint. He pumped his legs as fast as they would go. The yapping, snapping, and growling were getting closer. They seemed to be right on his heels. He broke out of the forest and glanced over his shoulder just in time to see a massive wolf bearing down on him. Thomas tripped and sprawled on the rough ground. He glanced again as the wolf leaped. Its fanged jaws opened, and red tongue lolled. Thomas braced and then heard a twang and a whoosh! The wolf crashed on him and lay still. Another twang and bark and whine, and it was silent.

The weight and smell of the massive wolf were over-whelming, but Thomas was powerless to move it. He looked to the side and spied leather boots. Deacon placed his boot on the body of the dead wolf and heaved, and it rolled off Thomas. An arrow pierced what Thomas assumed would be its heart. Thomas gazed up at Deacon, who stood like a statue holding a yew bow. Grateful to be alive, Thomas sputtered, "Deacon, thank you... I'm so sorry!"

Deacon considered the boy for a moment and then turned and walked away.

————

The climb back up the cliff was miserable in the cold darkness. Thorn was waiting at the base of the cliff, and Deacon mounted the dragon, and they winged their way back to their campsite, leaving Thomas behind to consider the results of his rash decision as he struggled back up the rock face. His mother had often discussed his anger with him, and he resolved once again to grow up.

Thomas finally crested the cliff and trudged slowly to

the glowing mouth of the cave. The campfire had been stoked and burned cheerily. He looked toward Deacon and saw only his back toward the fire again. Thomas opened his mouth to say something and then heard a snore come from the rider.

Thomas laid down and pulled up his blanket. He shivered once and then felt the great dragon's wing stretched over him, protectively providing warmth. And he slept.

Chapter 30

Deacon was busy loading Thorn's saddlebags.

Thomas shivered and jumped to his feet. He slapped at his body, trying to warm up.

"It's freezing!"

Deacon continued loading the saddlebag. His back was stiff and as straight as a ramrod. *I guess he's still mad about last night*, thought Thomas.

Thorn swung his head from Thomas to Deacon and rumbled at his rider.

Deacon's shoulders relaxed a bit, and he said, "There's still a big mug of hot kava in the embers… and this might help."

Deacon pulled something from the saddlebag. As he turned, Thomas saw that it was a leather riding jacket. Deacon stopped and did something Thomas thought was quite odd.

The rider brought the jacket up to his nose, then inhaled deeply—especially across the fur-lined collar. Thomas stood quietly, mystified at this ritual. Then

Deacon walked the coat over to the boy and placed it on his shoulders.

Thomas quickly slipped it on, snuggling into its fur lining. "Wow, this fits perfectly!" he said, as he rubbed its smooth, well-oiled leather.

"I thought it would," said Deacon as he stepped back to Thorn. He swung his leg over the beast, settled into the saddle, then offered his hand to help Thomas up.

Realizing, Thomas used what was left of the kava to douse the fire's embers, dropped the mug into the open bag, pulled it closed, tied the lash tight, then accepted Deacon's outstretched hand and was quickly in his place behind him.

"Where did you get this?" he queried, still admiring the leather riding jacket.

"It belonged to someone," Deacon responded

"Who?"

"Someone."

Thomas decided to drop it. "Thanks." Thomas admired the leather gloves Deacon was wearing as he rubbed his own hands to warm them. "You think I could get some of those?"

Deacon looked down at his well-worn gloves. "These? You have to earn these."

Deacon nudged the big dragon's flanks. "Up, Thorn."

Thorn sprung off the cliff ledge, extended his wings and glided off.

Chapter 31

Deacon expertly pulled the reins of his reptilian steed with his leather gloved hands, steering their glide through the clouds. Thomas now sat in front of Deacon, all his fear of flying gone.

Thomas looked out through the early morning mist; the dragon's speed made the drops sting Thomas's face. He didn't care, though, because he was taking in a majestic vista that stretched out under him as far as his eyes could see.

What was the line from that song he loved to sing back in his American school? Oh yes!

> *"O beautiful for spacious skies,*
> *for amber waves of grain;*
> *for purple mountains' majesties,*
> *Above the fruited plain..."*

That was precisely what he was experiencing now.

As Thomas thought of his old school in America, his mind naturally went from there to his American school bus to a sudden memory of him walking home up the old road after getting off the bus.

There was the old wooden house with the big tree in the front yard, and the wide porch, then the screen door opened and out walked his mother... and then his father. They embraced each other, then both smiled at him and waved welcoming him home.

And at that moment, Thomas felt his heart might break. *How can you go, in such a quick second, from such joy to such pain?* He longed to be home. He wanted to find his father. But he was a long, long way from home.

Snap out of it, he told himself. And he unconsciously shook his head, willing the memories away. He turned his thoughts to Deacon instead and chose to think of the fun they had had last night around the fire. And then he remembered his foolhardy attempt to run away.

Thomas cleared his throat. "I'm sorry about last night."

"Huh?" Deacon responded.

"I was stupid."

"Yes, you were," Deacon shifted in the saddle. "You could have been killed."

Thomas remembered all the fatherly talks he had received from his Dad then looked over his shoulder at Deacon.

"You remind me of my dad, sometimes."

Deacon was taken aback by this sudden show of intimacy.

He peered off into the distance. "You remind me of..." Deacon's voice trailed off. At this moment, Thomas thought, *He looks like I must have looked just moments ago when memories flooded in, and I had to chase them away or cry.*

Banishing those thoughts, Thomas followed up his statement about his father: "I mean, I've never seen my dad fight like you. In fact, I've never seen him fight at all. I don't know if he can even hold a sword. Well, we do have a sword. But it's an antique, and it hangs in his office. I mean, we have a lot of fun together. You'll like him."

Deacon responded by offering the dragon's reins to Thomas.

"Here, give it a try."

Thomas stared at the reins like they were hot.

"I... better not."

Deacon pushed them into Thomas's hands.

"Come on."

Thomas hesitated one more moment, then gave in. He gingerly took the reins from Deacon's leather-gloved hands.

Thomas held the reins limply and asked: "How am I doing?"

Thorn moaned.

"Very daring. Give him a little encouragement."

Thomas looked at Deacon quizzically.

"Give him a little kick." Deacon explained.

Thomas's heels barely nudged the dragon's flanks.

Thorn groaned.

"Come on, boy—this is your chance to fly a dragon!"

A fire kindled in Thomas's eyes, and a crazy grin spread across his face. He let out a "Whoop!" and kicked the dragon with all his might.

Thorn took off.

Thomas tilted backward from the dragon's sudden surge of power, which caused Thomas to pull up on the reins, which caused the direction-following Thorn to angle almost vertically into the sky.

"Wow!" Thomas exclaimed as he fell against Deacon's chest.

"Take it easy," laughed the man "and pull him down a bit!"

"Huh?"

The dragon continued to soar straight up.

"Down! Pull the reins down, Thomas!"

"Ah!" Thomas complied, excited at his power to direct Thorn. But in his excitement, he overcompensated at pulling the reins down. Ever obedient to his rider's guidance, the great dragon stalled in mid-air, then folded his wings back and dove.

"AayeeEEE!" Thomas screamed as the ground rushed to meet them.

"Give me the reins!" demanded Deacon.

Expertly, Deacon pulled up on the reins just enough that Thorn quickly leveled off, and he trumpeted, sensing the renewed touch of his master's hand. The great dragon glided smoothly over the beautiful grassy plains.

Eyes wide with excitement, Thomas looked up at his friend and exclaimed: "Let's do it again!"

"No," said Deacon, who looked a little pale, "I think that's enough flying lessons for today."

"Aww, come on!" Thomas said sullenly.

But Deacon firmly said: "We really need to move on."

Thorn snorted. It sounded a bit like a smirking chortle.

"Yes, I feel fine," Deacon shot back. "And mind your own business."

But Thomas was now oblivious because his eyes had become captivated at the beautiful valley that stretched below. So vibrant. So breathtaking. Thomas looked to the east, and there in the distance stood massive gray mountains reaching to the sky like sharp fangs. Here and there, snow glinted reflecting the sun. The summit was covered in a swirling dark cloud.

Thomas pointed. "What are those mountains?"

Deacon squinted, "Those are the Forbidden Range. Strange people live there, and our kind is not welcome."

Deacon indicated the cloud covering the summit. "The upper peaks are covered in a perpetual storm."

How cold that place must be, Thomas thought. *What kind of people could possibly live in that frostbitten land?* Thomas shivered.

He tore his gaze away from the Forbidden Lands and looked at a more pleasant scene before them. Another range but more inviting.

"Are we almost there?" Thomas asked

"Just over the next mountain range," Deacon said with a sigh.

Chapter 32

As those snow-capped peaks loomed nearer, Thomas scanned them for signs of Deacon's settlement. He also hoped they gained altitude because they seemed on a collision course with a large and high exposed-rock cliff.

Then Thomas realized they were climbing, and that the thinner air was making Thorn's heart, lungs, and wings work much harder to gain the needed elevation.

Thomas hoped against hope as he wondered: *Could we be aiming even higher than this mighty beast can handle?*

The giant dragon's breath matched the faster beating of his wings; each hot exhale created a puff of cloud in the frigid air.

Thomas shivered and pulled the fur collar of his leather jacket closer around his neck. Down near the plains, he thought it was overkill to have such a coat. But now, he was thankful for its warmth.

Looking forward again, Thomas felt like the approaching, sheer cliff face went up forever. For a moment, Thomas feared that Thorn was going to fly them straight into the granite.

Then Thomas's eyes adjusted, to the whites and grays and blues of the snow and rock and sun and shadow, and he saw that to the left side of the nearest cliff-face, there was a slight backward jog in the mountain behind that cliff face before a further-back granite wall resumed.

And as Thorn flew very close to that backward jog, then took a sharp right, Thomas saw they were facing the opening to a deep, narrow, U-shaped canyon that angled in behind the foreboding cliff. A hidden slot, if you like, behind what seemed to be an impenetrable wall until you got directly up to it.

Thorn angled for the bottom of the narrow U—so tight that as they flew in, Thomas noticed that Thorn's wingtips were brushing snow off the canyon's walls.

But then the thin passage opened up, and they emerged into a beautiful full canyon with a vast green valley on its floor. Thomas now noticed that there were hewn out dwellings up in the canyon walls. Déjà vu. He felt he had seen this before.

Then he remembered: It reminded him of a book he read in school about the Anasazi Indians of Arizona!

As they neared that populated canyon wall, Thomas could make out dragons perched along an outcropping. Now he could see people busily going about their day. This was a bustling village, built into the cliffs.

Thorn glided over the valley floor, and Thomas spotted a river of dark blue running right down its center. And now he also saw distinct patches of different greens arranged in rectangles and squares. Thomas realized they were crops. Wow! Cliff dwellers, dragon-riders, farmers…

Thomas turned in amazement and said to Deacon over his shoulder: "What do you call this place?"

Deacon didn't answer for a moment; he was surveying

the beautiful landscape below them. Finally, he said: "Home. We just call it 'Home.'"

Chapter 33

Ellie stopped work for a moment. She leaned on her hoe, pushed her riotous red curls back from her face, and brushed some dust off her calf-length wool tunic. She took a deep breath: new grass, freshly tilled earth. These were the smells of their hidden stronghold.

She had passed twenty-two harvests just last month, and her attractive features gave plenty of young men in the Home good reason to try their hand at courting her.

But she was determined not to court any man she could best in farming, swordplay, or dragon-riding. So there were few courters. In fact, only one man stood a chance.

A shadow passed over her. The bugle-call of a dragon echoed off the canyon walls.

Ellie shaded her eyes from the afternoon sun, peered up at the dragon and his riders.

"Deacon," she whispered to herself. Dropping her hoe, she sprinted across the furrowed rows to intersect with the landing.

Loren smiled to see his daughter run to meet Deacon;

this smile only deepened the fissures in his sun-browned face. The youngest of Loren's many children, Ellie, was the gift given him late in life. But it was a bittersweet, for Ellie's hard birth had cost the life of Fee, his dear wife.

On a full shelf along the canyon wall, a big rider named John tended a huge brown dragon. He was the oldest son of Loren. Dressed in more extended versions of the same leather jacket and britches that Deacon typically wore, John was an imposing sight to any enemy, but a welcome sight to any friend.

Hearing Thorn's bugle, John turned, smiling, from rubbing down his own giant beast. John then turned back, gave his dragon two more strokes, and a grateful pat, then descended the stone stairs that were carved into the canyon walls.

Chapter 34

Thorn glided in broad spirals, slowly descending until he landed gently in a meadow on the valley's floor.

Deacon helped Thomas slide down off Thorn's back, then turned to retrieve something from his saddlebags. But feeling Thomas's tugging at his trouser leg, Deacon turned around... just as Ellie came fully into view.

"Deacon!"

Deacon and Thomas exchanged glances. "Oh no," Deacon muttered under his breath.

Thorn trumpeted. Deacon gave Thorn a loving slap.

"Yeah, maybe she's not so bad."

Deacon dismounted. "Then again, she doesn't feed me venison and honey."

Thorn stared at his master; the beast gave a growl like distant thunder.

Ellie reached the dragon and his two riders.

"Hello, Deacon."

Deacon continued, unlashing Thorn's saddle.

"Hello, Ellie. And Ellie," Deacon nodded at the boy, "this is Thomas."

Ellie and Thomas considered each other. Thomas was not sure whether to shake hands or bow. So he just gave the attractive redhead a goofy grin.

Ellie gave an almost-curtsy to Thomas; to him, it seemed both strong and feminine.

Then, turning back to Deacon, Ellie asked with bright eyes: "Can I help ya, Deacon?"

His back to Ellie because he was still releasing the saddle, Deacon grinned at Thomas before he said: "Well now, lass, you might just can." She stepped forward to hear more.

And at just that moment, Deacon jerked the saddle off Thorn's back, spun around, and maneuvered so he could plop the big saddle right into Ellie's arms. "You can clean and polish that," Deacon said. "Can't ya, little girl?"

She wobbled under the weight but made no sound. Thomas noticed, though, that her blazing eyes communicated plenty.

Pleased with himself, Deacon patted her on the head and walked away. He called back over his shoulder: "Thanks, Ellie! Thomas, you coming or not?"

"Nice to meet you," Thomas shouted backwards as he ran to catch up.

Ellie stood, grimacing under the weight of the saddle. Her eyes shooting darts into Deacon's back. Then, with an "oof!" she slowly collapsed into a cloud of leather and dust.

Thomas stole another glance back at Ellie, as she now struggled to stand back up with Deacon's rig.

"She's pretty..."

Deacon ignored the boy's comment, continued marching toward the cliff dwellings along the canyon wall. From those dwellings, Loren and John came out to meet them.

"... In a tough sort of way." Thomas looked at Deacon, who gave no evidence he even knew the boy existed.

"And that hair—"

"Mind your own business," Deacon said flatly.

"Oooo... you like her!" Thomas thought of one of his friends back in America. That kid had a crush on a girl in their class, and everyone in the school knew the boy liked the girl. But the kid would have resisted to the death before he would ever admit it.

Funny, thought Thomas, as he looked up at the hardened warrior walking beside him. *That kid was in seventh grade, this guy's ancient like, thirty-something. I guess guys don't really change much over time.*

They reached Loren and John. There were embraces, with a lot of manly backslapping.

"Still pestering my baby sister?" John said with a wry grin.

"She likes it."

John cocked an eyebrow and smiled.

"I know she's no, Emma, but... You know it's been almost 5 years."

"Hey, don't you start too," Deacon responded.

John knew when to back off. He turned to Thomas: "You look a lot better'n the last time I saw you."

The last time? The last time I was running for my life from giant dark shadow monsters in my singed pajamas, thought Thomas. A shiver ran through him as he remembered the horror of that night.

Thomas smiled at the big man.

"Thomas," said Deacon, "this is John and Loren."

"Pleased to meet you, Thomas." Loren bowed formally, then shook Thomas's hand. "Quite a grip you've got there, son," Loren said. Then he noticed the leather riding jacket that Thomas wore. That made him pause.

"And that is a fine looking riding jacket." Loren rested both hands on the boy's shoulders. Momentarily lost in thought.

"Yeah, Deacon let me wear it." Thomas responded.

"He did, did he?" Loren glanced at Deacon, who shrugged.

Loren finally released Thomas, and to Deacon said, "After that long ride, I'd wager some ale is in order, eh?"

Deacon slapped him on the back. "You don't have to ask me twice."

Chapter 35

Loren poured ale into earthen mugs. He even splashed a little into Thomas's cup, then diluted it with water. Deacon sat with his boots propped on a low table. Thomas found a chair and sat holding his mug in both hands. As the men drank, the mood grew somber.

"John told me about Simon," said Loren. "A mighty rider he was, and a true friend... a great loss."

Deacon nodded and raised his mug solemnly. The others did the same.

"To Simon."

"To Simon!" the others responded, then each grew quiet reflecting on their friend.

Finally, Deacon broke the silence.

"Loren," said Deacon, "Thomas has quite a story to tell."

Loren took a gulp of his ale, all the while gazing at Thomas. "Does he now?"

Thomas followed suit and sipped his ale. His eyes bulged as the elixir burned down the back of his throat. He swallowed and replied hoarsely: "I'm not... from around here."

Chapter 36

Thorn's saddle was thrown in a heap on the stable's stone floor. The floor was worn smooth from years of use by dragons and their riders.

Considering the pile of dusty saddle leather, Ellie wiped the sweat off her forehead and contemplated the hours of cleaning and polishing ahead of her.

She decided the saddle could wait. Instead, she grabbed a sizable coarse-haired brush and turned to Thorn, who was contentedly eating from a trough.

"Doesn't he ever give you a bath?" she said as she began brushing the great dragon's golden hide.

Thorn rumbled in response.

"I didn't think so."

Ellie brushed with more vigor.

"Who does he think I am? His stable girl? Well, I've got news for him..."

The more she thought about it, the angrier she got.

"I'm sick to death of his condescending attitude," she said, now brushing Thorn's hide furiously. "And I won't stand for it anymore! Not one moment more!"

Annoyed at this maltreatment, Thorn turned his head and huffed his nostrils at Ellie.

"Oh, sorry, Thorn! I know he's not your fault." Self-consciously, she lightened her brushing touch.

"That better?"

Thorn groaned and jerked his head to guide her brushing upward.

"Oh. Behind your shoulder?"

Ellie moved her brushing. And the big dragon closed his eyes with a moan-growl of contentment.

"A little to the left?"

Thorn's hind leg began to paw the air like a big reptile dog. Ellie laughed and gently scratched the big dragon's chin.

"Thanks for listening."

Chapter 37

Thomas placed his mug on the low table. He had spent the last hour telling the men how he had followed his father through the Mairead Fhada portal. Loren had sat quite still the whole time, listening with his fingers steepled and his eyes half-closed.

At points in the story, Thomas wondered if the old man was asleep. But then he would prompt Thomas with a quiet "Continue."

Loren and John sat across from the boy; Deacon stood leaning against the timber mantel over the stone fireplace.

"Then John and Deacon rescued me from the shadow warriors," Thomas finished, then said, "Oh, Deacon, tell them about the shadow warriors in town."

"They," responded Deacon, "have heard more than enough of my stories." Then Deacon turned to Loren. "What do you think of it all?"

Loren didn't respond; he just leveled his gaze on Thomas and sat silent, for what seemed to Thomas like an eternity. He shifted his feet uncomfortably, feeling like he was back in the headmaster's office.

"Quite a story, eh?" said John, breaking the silence.

Thomas broke with Loren's gaze and stared at the floor. "You don't believe me," he said with a sigh.

"Oh, we believe you," the old man reassured.

"You do?"

"You see, your father was not the first person through that door."

As Thomas's brow furrowed with curiosity, Loren retrieved his cane, and with a groan, got up from his chair. "Let me show you something." Loren made his way to a rustic shelf overstuffed with ancient books and scrolls. He searched and eventually found what he was looking for. He pulled out a large, worn, leather book, then brought it and clearing a spot of parchment papers, quills, and ink containers set it on the table between them.

Loren opened the book, sending a cloud of dust into the air. The Elder mumbled as he read, tracking the page with his finger, searching for a specific passage. "Ah, here it is." He cleared his throat and read aloud:

> *"When the veil is thin*
> *and the warrior is armed*
> *walk the path of the Creator*
> *But be warned*
> *Destruction awaits he*
> *Who steps to the right or left."*

Loren continued, "And in that time, those of our world and Otherland may cross the threshold and set foot on the other side. And on the thirty-first turn, the door shall be closed. Take heed, lest the traveler be caught unaware."

Deacon and John sat quietly.

Thomas looked back and forth between them, bewildered.

"So, what does it mean?"

"The portal you call Mairead Fhada can only be opened during a specific season when the stars are aligned precisely, and the traveler walks the path of the Creator. Otherlanders like you and your father have stumbled into our land. In the same way, some of our people have passed through and never returned. Still, others tried to pass and were destroyed."

Deacon looked at Thomas. "You were lucky," he said, leaning forward.

"No,"corrected Loren, "You were blessed. The ancients put the marking stones at the threshold to warn us: 'Beware, there is danger here.'"

Thomas stood and peered at the words in the book. He couldn't make out the ancient ruins, but he pointed to the verse. "Can you reread this part, Please sir."

Loren considered the boy. Then read:

> *"When the veil is thin*
> *and the warrior is armed*
> *walk the path of the Creator*
> *But be warned*
> *Destruction awaits he*
> *Who steps to the right or left."*

"I know what the path of the creator is," Thomas said quietly.

"Go on." The old man encouraged.

Thomas took one of the sheets of parchment and a quill. He thought for a moment, then dipped the feather in the inkpot and drew a circle. He inked the quill again and drew three matching intertwined leaves: The Trinitarian Celtic Circle.

Thomas dropped the quill back in the inkpot and straightened up.

Loren stared at the drawing. "This is the symbol of the Creator. Where did you see this?"

"Wait," Thomas reached into the front pocket of his britches. "I forgot I still had this!"

He pulled out a charred folded fragment of paper. He unfolded it and laid it on the table, smoothing out the wrinkles as best he could.

"This is how I came here."

Loren stood and picked up the charred fragment. "Yes'" he said, looking at Deacon and John. "And that must be how the others came here as well."

"Others?" Thomas asked.

Loren handed the fragment back to Thomas and picked up the ancient book and slid it back in its place as he continued:

"There was another who came through the door many decades ago, and he brought great darkness with him. Darcon. He allied himself with the Shadow World and with their help, spread his rule over our once peaceful kingdom. His is a deep seated lust for power. Enough is never enough. He must be resisted at every point."

"But what about my father?" Thomas pleaded.

Deacon looked at his young friend with compassion. "Thomas, we anticipated someone coming through the door. We were going to be waiting and ready to meet the traveler. But our efforts were to no avail. Our scouts guarding the door were ambushed, killed—all but one. He passed later, but not before telling us what he saw."

"My father?"

"A stranger came through the door... and yes, it could have been your father."

Thomas stood. "Then where is he?" he asked in despair.

Deacon and John looked at each other, both weighing how to tell the boy the news.

Deacon nodded, and John leaned forward, "With Darcon."

Loren looked down at Thomas. "If it is your father, and if he knows the secret to the door, he is in great danger."

Chapter 38

Daniel Colson surveyed the stacks of scrolls and parchments before him with a sense of growing dread. He stood and scratched his beard. *I miss my razor*, he thought morosely. Daniel moved toward the small window set high in his prison wall. There was no glass. It seemed it had not been invented in this world yet. Also, the window was just a two-foot square opening in the thick stone wall, no bars. That was what the iron shackle was for.

Daniel took seven steps until the chain locked to his ankle went taut. The sunlight streamed through, lighting Daniel's dim cell. He peered longingly toward the bright window and lifted his hand into the sun's rays. His fingers could just barely reach into the light and feel the warmth.

He pulled futilely on his fetter, trying to get closer. It was useless. The chain was secured to an iron ring in the stone floor with a large padlock, and no attempt at dislodging it had even made it budge. Still, he had to try. Not to pull against his chain would mean to give up. Giving up would mean he would never go home. Never see his beautiful Caroline or his boy, Thomas. He gave the chain one last pull, straining with all his might. He tugged until he thought his heart would explode then dropped to the floor, panting. He lay there staring up at the ceiling as a strange spider-like creature crawled along it defying gravity.

How long had he been here? How long since his vain attempt to stop Albright? It was twenty-one days since he left his home and family and came through Mairead Fhada, the stone circle that acted as a door to this strange world. "The Universe Next Door." Wasn't that the title of a book he read in college? First, he had solved the problem of the stone circle. It wasn't an archaic temple or an observatory but an astronomical gateway to another planet. Once he understood that, then, it was the matter of unlocking the door. That came in the form of an ancient combination based upon the Trinitarian Celtic circle.

He remembered the night that he had cracked the code. He was in his study rooms at Edinburgh, it was in the evening when it had finally come to him. The symbol could be overlaid on a satellite photo of the stone circle, Mairead Fhada. Each corner of the 3 leaves of the trinitarian knot pointed to 3 of the 69 stones that made up the 350-foot circle. Then he rotated it so that the leaf known as Spirit pointed to the most massive stone in the circle. The 12-foot tall monolith the Scottish called "Long Meg."

Now he knew "where" he just had to figure out the "when." And he knew exactly where to look.

He had run across the campus like a mad man to the research library. He quickly greeted the old night watchmen.

"Workin' late again, I see, Professor."

"Yes, Tisdale, again." He responded as he scratched his name on the sign-in log.

Tisdale helpfully passed Daniel a pair of white cotton

gloves for handling the artifacts. Slipping them on, he rushed up and down the ancient collections until he found what he was searching for. An ancient Celtic illuminated manuscript dated in the 900's AD. He placed it on a table and carefully turned through the pages. He stopped. A crude map of the stone circle "Long Meg and her Daughters" and above it the stars represented in gold in the shape of the consolation Orion.

Daniel pulled out his small, well-worn leather notebook. He preferred to do things the old school way. Paper and a fountain pen.

He thumbed through pages of scribbled notes. Finding a blank page, he quickly sketched a diagram of the stone circle and the constellation of stars found in the ancient book.

Then, Daniel snapped a picture with his phone and ran back to his office to find his 28-year-old doctoral assistant, Albright pouring over his notes.

"I've done it, Albright!" He remembered shouting in his excitement and sat at his computer and proceeded to print the photo from his office printer. Then he accessed an astronomical charts website. Albright stooped over him as Daniel blathered on in his excitement. "All the years of continuous research. The late nights and early mornings, all the hours spent in dusty libraries and in the fields digging in the cold mud of rural Britain. It's finally paying off."

Albright straightened his tall frame and pushed his blond locks out of his eyes. "I guess congratulations are in order Professor." Albright had said heartily.

But now Daniel remembered a strange look in his assistants' eyes and how his smile seemed cold.

"It's a door, Albright. A gate. A portal! And according to my calculations it is open..." he had swiveled the computer screen to Albright emblazoned with the constellation Orion and the month October. "This month."

"Amazing," Albright whispered. "Dr. Colson, how does, are you sure, could it…?"

"Not now, Albright, we have plenty of time to write this all up and present my paper at the Archeologist society in two months. "I've done it. I've really done it!

Daniel remembered how Albright tried to have his questions answered, but Daniel had cut him off.

"Not now, Albright!" He had shouted impatiently. "I must tell my wife."

He stepped outside to call Caroline and tell her the news. He couldn't get a signal with his cell phone. He ended the call in frustration but then remembered that on the top floor of an adjacent building, he had had reception.

The professor bounded up the steps and attempted the call only to hear his wife's message. He left a message and came back out of breath into his office. "Well, Albright, I owe you…" He stopped. The office was empty. Albright was gone, along with his research!

In the dank cell Daniel shivered, laying on the cold stone floor of his prison. He sat up and rubbed his ankle where the iron cuff had worn a sore and prayed that it wasn't infected. He stood and sat back at the wooden table piled high with the tomes of this world. His laptop sat cold and lifeless beside it. "Should have brought an extra battery." He said aloud to no-one. There were a lot of things he should've done differently.

He shouldn't be here. He never should have come. But he was driven by rage when he realized that his assistant, Albright, had stolen his research.

That night Daniel had wondered what Albright could possibly do with his research. Publish it? Play it off as his own? Then he knew. Albright was going to the stone circle, Mairead Fhada, in Cumbria, the focus of all of Daniel's years of work.

He had grabbed his leather satchel, stuffed a few things in it that he might need. He made one stop before leaving the college and slipped into the research library past the sleeping Tisdale and grabbed the 900 AD manuscript. He felt guilty about it, but he had a feeling he might need it. Then he raced after his assistant. He didn't know what he would do if he caught him. It was his research, his alone, and he would take it back no matter what.

Now in the cold, dim cell as he relived those rash decisions, he was overcome with sincere regret. His stupid pride and anger had caused him to leave behind the two most important people in his world. Daniel lay his head on the wooden table and whispered a prayer for his wife and their son.

Chapter 39

"This place gives me quite the fright," whispered the Weasel to himself twitching. He had made his way to this place with information to sell. That was the way he made his way in this dark world. Trading on human suffering. He had held the young serving girl captive by threatening her poor old mother. She had sold out her own people for the love of her "dear old Ma." The old hag probably wouldn't live long anyway. He had no room in his heart for anyone but himself. He twitched and continued his pacing nervously up and down in Darcon's fortress courtyard. After two more revolutions, he stopped and squinted up at the battlements.

Guards stood with their crossbows, and watchful eyes, trained on him. He turned to continue his pacing and gave a squeak of surprise. He had almost smashed into the iron breastplate of General Nawg, the massive shadow-warrior commander.

"You have something for me?" demanded Nawg.

"Ah, yes. Rumor, I understand, has it your lordship is looking for a boy?" Weasel looked back and forth, then leaned into the dark warrior and lowered his voice: "An Otherlander..."

"Go on."

"I've been trading in the middle region, and I've seen some things."

"Where is the boy?"

"Not so fast!" *This is going well*, thought Weasel. *This place isn't as scary as I thought. And now I've got this brute right where I want him.* "I say, always leave some room for negotiation." Weasel turned to the General. "And if it goes well, I also have a location for the right price."

Nawg stood silently, stonily glaring at the jerky little man. His black-gloved hand moved to his huge sword's hilt, and Weasel began to think he had overplayed his hand. With a twitch, he snuck a glance up at the guards; their deadly weapons were still trained on him.

A cold drip of sweat rolled down his spine; he shivered. But he reminded himself: *Wait, I know how these barters work: The first one to talk, loses.*

Nawg regarded the pathetic little man deciding whether to listen more or cleave him in two with his blade. Finally, "Follow me," commanded Nawg.

Perfect—I've got him right where I want him, thought Weasel, as he followed General Nawg through a dark opening that became a passage through the fortress's wall. They were soon swallowed by darkness.

Chapter 40

The jingling of keys awakened Daniel. His head hurt. Not enough food and water would do that. He glanced up at his open window. The moon had risen and cast a faint light into his cell. The rusty lever of the door turned with a screech, and the massive door swung open. Daniel could just make out the backs of the hulking guards standing in the corridor.

A servant girl stepped inside, holding a candle. She moved like a frightened mouse as she lit the few torches in Daniel's cell. Daniel smiled at her. She was the only bright spot in the dreary days of his captivity. Then she retreated to the side of the door giving a bow and averting her gaze as Mordis Saldan entered.

He was thin and older than Daniel. Hard to tell his age. His head was clean-shaven, but his face sprouted a massive gray beard that had been braided into a single cord. *He was vain like that*, Daniel thought. His black cassock fit tight and had a high collar. Each button down the front shown in the candlelight like drops of fire, but his eyes did not. They gave off nothing. They seemed to absorb the light.

"Dr. Colson," he said as he entered.

Daniel sat resolutely. He had tired of these daily interrogations.

"Why are you here?" Mordis asked.

"I've told you already."

"Tell us again."

Daniel sighed. "I came looking for my assistant. Gavin Albright. Young, fit, blonde, almost 30, and smart, very smart. He would have come here only hours before I arrived."

Mordis stroked his braided beard. "There was a man as you describe." Mordis let that hang in the air. "But he is no more." He turned to gaze out the open window at the moon.

"My Lord Darcon request your access to the door."

Daniel spat back in frustration. "I have told you I don't know how to get back. The pattern is probably the same on the lock, but the constellations are all different in your world."

"My Lord, Darcon request access to the door," Mordis repeated flatly.

Daniel looked around the cell in desperation.

"I don't know how to go back through the door. Don't you realize I more than anyone want to get back through that door! My world, my home, my family is on the other side."

"Well, you must try harder."

"Look! You have beaten me, chained me like an animal. What more can you do to me?"

"You are right, we cannot do more to you without losing you."

Mordis hand shot out and snatched the servant girl by the arm, and to her horror pulled her slowly toward him.

"Hey! Leave her alone!" Daniel demanded.

The servant girl snuck a pleading glance toward Daniel then cast her eyes to the floor as her master straightened out her arm and reached with his other hand to retrieve a lit candle from the wall.

Daniel lunged toward Mordis, but his chain held tight. He clawed at the monster, but Mordis stood inches away from his grasp.

Mordis leveled his cold gaze on Daniel as he held the burning candle over the trembling girl's exposed forearm, threatening to pour the hot wax there.

The girl bit her lip, preparing for the pain as tears sprung from her eyes.

"Stop!" Daniel pleaded. "Please stop!"

Mordis released the girl, and she shrank back against the wall into the shadows. Then slipped through the door, sneaking one glance at Daniel as if to communicate, "Thank you."

Mordis turned and moved out the door then paused. "Dr. Colson, resume your studies. Lord Darcon is a patient man. But his patience has its limits."

The door slammed, and Daniel shuffled back to the table, his chain clanged along behind him. He crumpled into his chair and stared at the research before him. He opened his notebook, and referring to his scattered research began to write. He would solve the problem of the door. He had no choice. He had to get home. But how without allowing the darkness of this world to seep through to his?

Chapter 41

Mordis Saldan entered Darcon's inner sanctuary in silence. As he walked between the phalanx of the place guard, only his cassock made a quiet hiss along the floor. He stopped at the foot of the dais and bowed.

"My Lord."

His dark Master ignored him. Darcon stared into his hand, at something he held there, lost deep in thought.

Mordis cleared his throat. "My Lord?"

Darcon looked up and focused on Mordis. His eyes registered something distant then flashed anger at having been disturbed. He slipped the small piece of what looked to Mordis like parchment into the folds of his robe.

Lord Darcon stood, stepped forward, and looked down upon his loyal counselor. "Well?"

"Still nothing, Master. He knows how he came through the door but does not know how to return."

"Like the other one?"

"Yes, Sire, like the other one."

"And what of the boy? Or the location of the resistance strongholds?"

"We are making progress there." Mordis said with a smile."

"Good. Once we have destroyed the resistance and rule this world, we will move on to the next."

Mordis turned to leave.

"Mordis."

"Yes, my Lord?"

"Bring him to me."

"Sire?"

"The man of learning. This traveler. Have him brought to my table tonight." Darcon smiled. "Maybe my hospitality will help things along."

Modis bowed. "As you wish."

Chapter 42

Keys jingled, and the lever screeched, alerting Daniel that the door to his cell was about to open. A moment of indecision, and then he stood and picked up his chair and stepped toward the door as it cracked. Daniel lifted the chair above his head as someone stepped through. Daniel stopped mid-swing and set the chair on the floor. It was the servant girl. She was holding a mug of water and a loaf of bread. As Daniel stepped forward, the girl caught his eye for a moment then quickly looked to the floor.

"Sir, I have brought you food and water."

"Thank you," He said as he took it and placed it on the table.

The girl backed to the door, her head to the floor submissively.

"Please, miss, what is your name?" Daniel asked gently.

She stopped unsure of herself. Unaccustomed to receiving even the smallest act of kindness.

"Mia." She softly said to the floor.

"Mia. That's a nice name."

He stepped toward the door as she continued backing.

Daniel intended to get the door for her, but he reached the end of his chain. Looking from his shackle to the girl. "Forgot," he said, shrugging his shoulders and lifting his chained ankle. "This is as far as I go."

The girl opened the door and began to step through, then paused long enough to whisper, "Thank you."

Chapter 43

"How long until they find us?" Deacon slammed his hand onto the wooden table, which echoed through the council chamber. He glared at the gathered men, the leaders of the resistance, and the elders of "Home."

An elder stood and stepped from behind the intricately carved conference table. He spoke to Deacon but faced the gathering. "Deacon, friend we are secure here in our valley hidden within the mountains." He turned to face Deacon. "Our pass is protected by sentries. Our Dragons are strong and swift. Let us hear no more talk of war." Some of the gathered men and women nodded their heads and murmured their assent.

Deacon shot back. "Gindar, brother, you have been lulled into complacency by what you believe is security. It is only a matter of time before Darcon's forces find us. We must strike now and take the battle to Darcon's doorsteps. We cannot afford to lose any more of our men. We have given up too much that is precious."

Gindar nodded. "You, more than most, have sacrificed for our people. But now is not the time, and we are not prepared to go on the offense. And besides all that, this is the time of our annual feast. Let our people rejoice in the security of their Home."

Deacon started to respond, but Loren stood and raised his hand, stopping further discussion. "General Deacon. The council has heard your concerns."

Deacon opened his mouth then thought better of it. He nodded at Loren, turned on his heel, and marched out of the chamber.

Chapter 44

The door to Daniel's cell opened, and Mordis stepped through. "Professor, My Lord, Darcon requests your presence at his table tonight."

Daniel looked up from his research and took off his spectacles.

"Request or order?"

Mordis ignored the comment.

"Water has been brought and your other clothes. So that you may..." He sniffed the room with a grimace. "Prepare."

Mordis retreated past the guards as the servant girl, Mia, entered with a basin and a jar of water. She placed the bowl on the table and filled it with water. Steam rose into the cold air of the cell.

Mia snuck a glance at Daniel.

"I have heated the water."

Daniel, struck by her kindness, uttered," Thank you."

The servant girl stepped out, then back in with a parcel and handed it to him gently. Unwrapping it, Daniel found the jacket that he had worn when he had first arrived.

"I cleaned it for you," Mia explained.

Now Daniel didn't know what to say. He took the jacket and placed it on the back of his chair.

She looked down at his shackled ankle. "I will send the guard to unlock your-" She couldn't bring herself to say it.

Daniel, sensing her unease, responded softly, "It's okay. It's not your fault. You're as much a prisoner as I."

Mia bowed her head and backed out of the door.

Chapter 45

Daniel squinted at his research in the dim light of his cell. The cell door unlocked and swung open on its groaning hinges. Two prison guards were back along with Mia. She quietly lit the candles in Daniel's cell as one of the guards knelt and roughly grabbed Daniel's ankle.

"Careful," Daniel grimaced. Seeing his inflamed ankle, the guard stood and pulling an iron key out of a small leather bag hanging around his neck, he shoved it into Mia's hands and pushed her to the floor. "You do it," He growled. "I don't want to catch nothin'."

Mia gently took the key and unlocked the shackle, and it clanged to the floor.

Escorted by the servant girl and the two guards, Daniel walked along the torch-lit stone corridor. They rounded a bend, and Daniel stopped abruptly.

"What was I thinking? I forgot my jacket."

The servant girl moved to respond. "I will send for it."

"No, please. I'll just run back and get it." Before the guards could respond, he took off, darting back the way they had come. He rounded another corner, approached the door to his cell… and kept on running. He heard the shouts of the guards and their running steps echoing in the hall behind him.

Another two turns, and he was in a portion of the halls he had never seen. He stopped, unsure of himself. He could hear nothing but the faint fluttering of the lit torches.

Suddenly the silence was broken by a scream echoing through the passage. Startled, Daniel stopped and listened.

Maybe he was hearing things, he thought. He cautiously continued forward. As he approached an intersection of halls, the same voice screamed again. Daniel could tell it was coming from the adjoining hallway.

Daniel stood at the crossroad, debating what he should do. Finally, he moved down the hallway toward the sound of the screams.

Approaching a corner, he turned to see more halls. He continued along one hallway, and it divided. Unsure of which way to go, Daniel stopped. The screams had silenced.

He looked back the way he had come—he thought. Uncertain. And again, the doubts. *Why am I here? What have I got myself into*? With that, he turned to go back the way he was pretty sure he had come.

He hadn't taken one step when a very-close scream reverberated through the hallway—this time followed by indiscernible gibbering. Begging sobs. Words from someone in horrible pain. If Daniel listened intently, he could just make it out.

"Please," the voice pleaded, "That's all I know!"

Daniel apprehensively continued down the hallway toward the voice. Fear escalated. He looked over his shoulder and almost started to run away.

But in a moment of courage, he turned back purposefully and... bounced off the iron chest-plate of a shadow warrior. He looked up to see the dark visage of General Nawg.

Daniel stepped back to catch his breath.

"Excuse me," he said, trying to control his voice. "I didn't see you there."

General Nawg just stood, as silent and impervious as a granite wall.

"I... uh... got lost in the passageways. Is this the way to the dining hall?

Nothing.

"No," Daniel continued, "I see it is not." He backed away from the behemoth, with an, "I'm sure it was back this way." Then Daniel turned the way he had come. He looked back one last time. "Thank y—" Daniel didn't finish, for there was no one there. And just then, the two original guards came up from behind and grabbed him roughly by the arms, spun him around, and one punched him in the stomach, doubling him over. He fell to his knees gasping for breath.

The servant girl arrived, panting. "Sir, please!" she begged. Then she held up his jacket. "Your coat."

Daniel struggled to his feet. The guards seized him again, and Daniel violently shook them off, and took his jacket from the girl, slipped it on. "Forgive me," he groaned. "Let's not keep your master waiting."

Chapter 46

The darkness moved and turned. The being that was General Nawg stood in the flickering light of the chamber's single torch. His cloak didn't reflect the light but seemed to absorb it. Every room he entered was somehow darker because of his presence.

Lashed to a stone table lay the Weasel, trembling in fear.

Nawg moved to his victim. Leaning in, he said, "Now let us resume our negotiations."

Chapter 47

Daniel was shoved roughly through a door and tumbled to the floor. He jumped to his feet. "Hey!" He shouted as the door slammed in his face.

Daniel surveyed the room. It was a large stone hall: High vaulted ceiling, timbers, massive fireplace. It was then that Daniel realized he wasn't alone. At first, he thought they were statues. Standing ensconced along the walls were guards. They seemed to pay him no mind. These were not Shadow warriors but human men it seemed. Their bodies still draped in dark cloaks, and their chests emblazoned with the red symbol of Darcon, a circular crimson serpent writhing on an ebony background.

Daniel turned from the guards to study an ornate tapestry hanging on the wall of the great dining chamber.

The tapestry covered the whole south wall. It began at the far left in light, beautiful hues portraying green forests, floral fields, and a bright sun beaming down on peasant adults and children playing in communal joy.

Then, as it went to the right, it proceeded to darken in

both colors and content, gradually digressing from the pastoral to scenes of war, pillage, and deep anguish.

"You find it disturbing?" Darcon's voice echoed in the massive hall.

Daniel turned to see the dark lord approach—as usual, wearing his dark cloak, with a hood he kept raised to hide his face. A blood-red cape draped from his neck.

Daniel considered the lord's question for only a moment. "Yes. I do find it disturbing."

Darcon motioned at the scenes of war, "But it represents the truth of 'civilization,' always poised on the precipice of destruction. The weak ever needing the strong to show them the way. I find it invigorating."

Daniel pointed at the tapestry's anguished figures. "And how do they feel?"

Darcon said nothing in response, but Daniel chilled as he registered that under his hood, Darcon was smiling—if you could call it that.

Even though his lips curved upward, it was a dead, cold reaction. And he finally said, with a sneer in his voice, "My dear professor, without death there would be no life, progress, by its very nature, must always move forward. And you must move with it, or be crushed."

He paused, letting that last statement sink in. Then he clapped his hands and said, "Let's eat!"

Chapter 48

Darcon and Daniel faced each other over the long wooden dining table. Darcon continued to keep his hood on. That, and the flicker of the fire casting shadows, never allowed Daniel to really see his host's face. It was disconcerting to try and converse with someone when you couldn't see their eyes.

Darcon had finished his meal. He sat patiently as Daniel finished what looked like a large piece of grilled sirloin. It was all he could do not to pick up the piece and tear into it like a hungry dog. He was starving. He hadn't had meat in over a week.

"More wine," Darcon spoke barely over a whisper. A servant appeared instantly and filled Darcon's goblet.

Then the servant quietly came around behind Daniel and to his left. He extended the wine decanter and started to fill his glass. Daniel didn't realize the servant was there; he shifted in his seat and accidentally bumped the man's elbow. The decanter sloshed, and despite the servant's best effort, a single drop of wine fell to the table.

The servant paralyzed, watched in horror as the red

wine seeped into the white tablecloth, slowly growing a burgundy-red stain. Daniel, embarrassed, looked up to apologize.

But he froze when he locked eyes with the servant's and saw he was filled with absolute terror.

Darcon noticed the exchange.

"Really, it's only a drop of wine; there's plenty more where that came from. Do you require anything else, professor?"

"I'm fine."

"That will be all, man," Darcon said and dismissed him with a wave before turning back to his guest.

The servant breathed again. Then after one quick glance at Daniel, he rapidly departed.

"Dr. Colson, how is your research coming along?"

Daniel put his fork down. "I don't know how to go back through the door if that is what you mean?"

"If I can assist you in any way, please let me know."

Daniel considered the offer. "I would like to go outside for a walk or see the countryside. I must see the night sky to observe the constellations."

"That is out of the question, Dr. Colson." Darcon stood. "There are those who desire to do us harm. They roam the hills like vermin, attacking any of my people that are found alone. Remember that is what happened before we found you? You are fortunate we were there in time to save you."

Uneasy, Daniel shifted in his chair.

"I hate to think what would happen to you if you were ever out of your room alone."

The statement hung in the air. Daniel cleared his throat.

"You mean cell," he responded.

Darcon ignored the jab. "Dr. Colson, I need to know how to open the door."

"I'll tell you the same thing I've told Mordis for the last month. I don't know how to open it!"

Just then, an older male servant hurried in. He bent and whispered in Darcon's ear, and the man stiffened. Darcon dismissed the servant and stood.

"I am sorry. I have an important matter that requires my attention. Please excuse me. The servants will attend to your needs." Darcon paused. "And the guards will see you make it safely back to your room. Good night."

Daniel stood and watched Darcon leave. At least he was out of the cell for a while and had an actual meal. Daniel reached over and grabbed another hunk of bread off the table and a piece of fruit and shoved it in his jacket pocket just as the guards stepped forward and escorted Daniel toward the exit.

He surveyed the tapestry as he walked beside it. At the darkest end, the tapestry depicted the brutal aftermath of war: dozens of people crucified, and hundreds more lying slain on a full battlefield.

And standing on a hill, overseeing the slaughter, was an unmistakable representation of Daniel's host, Darcon.

Chapter 49

Darcon walked quickly down the passage, his cloak whipping behind him. He came to General Nawg, who stood silently at an intersection of the passages.

"General Nawg?"

"We have it, my lord. We know the location of their stronghold," said Nawg.

A wicked smile spread across Darcon's face.

And in a flurry of dark cloaks, they turned and continued down the passageway.

Chapter 50

The canyon floor was ablaze with torches and bonfires. The sounds of bagpipe-like instruments and fiddle-playing filled the night air with happy music. Thomas took another bite of the largest drumstick he had ever seen, then turned his attention back to the celebration.

It reminded him of the Renaissance Faire his family attended once, back in the States. Here, long tables formed a vast circle, around which a reveling congregation enjoyed a bounteous feast: steaming mounds of various meats and potatoes, and piles of fruits and vegetables.

Inside the circle of tables, men, women, and children engaged in a communal dance; it reminded Thomas of square-dancing.

"What do you think?" a deep male voice said.

Thomas turned to see Loren, who settled beside him.

"This is great!" Thomas exclaimed, watching the dance.

Deacon danced with a beautiful brunette partner. They joined hands with the rest of the merrymakers, and skipped in a joyous circle, then spun and skipped in the other direction. Then the circle broke, and Thomas couldn't help but laugh as he watched Deacon and his dancing partner spinning together.

"Deacon!" Thomas called, waving madly.

Hearing his name over the din, Deacon and the girl came dancing toward Thomas.

"Hello, Thomas!" Deacon called as they floated past. "Having fun?"

Thomas nodded crazily, causing Loren to laugh at the boy's joy.

"I wish I could dance like that!" exclaimed Thomas.

"You can," responded Loren with a smile. He then turned toward the dancers and called, "Ellie!"

Ellie wound her way through the dancers to Thomas and her father. Seeing her out of breath and glowing with joy, Thomas was struck by her beauty. He could only stammer, "No, I was just kidding."

"Ellie, our young guest would like to dance."

"No, no... I..."

Ignoring Thomas's protest, Ellie took his hand and dragged him into the circle.

"I don't dance," Thomas said as Ellie led him. "Well, not really, I sometimes jump around to music in my room by myself. But never," he gulped, "with a girl!"

Ellie smiled warmly at Thomas and pulled him to their starting place.

They joined hands with the rest of the dancers, as they formed another giant circle. The music started, and they all skipped to the right. Thomas was jerked awkwardly along by Ellie. As Thomas and Ellie came around to Loren, they saw Deacon and his dark-haired partner sitting that dance out. They laughed and waved to Thomas.

"Help!" Thomas mouthed, beseeching Deacon.

Deacon laughed, "You're doing great, boy!"

The circle reversed, and the whole happy throng skipped in the other direction.

Despite himself, Thomas laughed as he was pulled along by the circle and the beautiful redhead.

Chapter 51

Miles away, a huge storm brewed. Angry thunderheads built, and lightning arced from the rolling black clouds. And out of those black clouds surged a spreading stream of shadow warriors, astride their iron-clad dragons prepared for battle.

Chapter 52

Back in the fortress valley, Deacon smiled as he watched Ellie and Thomas dance. The circle broke, and couples spun off into their own orbits, still trying to hold close as they whirled and skipped and laughed.

Even as she led Thomas through the dance, Ellie felt someone watching her. She glanced in Deacon's direction, and sure enough, it was him. Their eyes locked for an awkward moment... then Ellie looked away despite herself.

Meanwhile, Thomas had utterly forgotten about his embarrassment. He was having a blast, dancing with a beautiful young woman! Thomas smiled at Ellie, relishing the moments until that song came to an end.

And almost immediately, Thomas felt a tap on his shoulder and turned to see an eager young man looking past him at the young redhead.

"Pardon me, sir, may I cut in?"

"Sure, okay," Thomas replied reluctantly.

Ellie turned to her young dancing partner, and with a curtsy, said, "Thank you, Thomas, for the dance. It was lovely." And a new song started.

Before Thomas could reply, she was swept away.

Thomas watched them go, then turned and walked out of the dancing circle. Every few steps, he did a little jig.

"Thank you, Thomas," he echoed Ellie, "the dance was lovely." Pretty pleased with himself, Thomas was. He scanned the rejoicing crowd, and something he saw froze him in his tracks. A woman in her thirties, and her son, about Thomas's age.

The sounds of the feast faded away. It could have been Thomas and his mother. The two looked through the crowd with delight. They were joined by a man who was obviously the boy's father. The father scooped up the boy and threw him over his shoulder, even though the boy felt he was too old for that.

Reality flooded back over Thomas. He stood stone-faced, oblivious to the merrymaking around him. Then he moved away from the dance to one of the bonfires at the edge of the gathering.

He stood there, staring into the flames until the tears came. Then he thought: *What am I doing? I came searching for my father. All this is a distraction.* He reached up and angrily wiped his tear-stained cheeks and turned with determination.

"Where is Deacon? He's got to help me."

Chapter 53

"No!" Deacon insisted, pushing through the crowd even as Thomas dogged him.

"But—"

"I said no." Deacon continued striding.

"You know where he is!" Thomas protested, running to catch up.

"It's dangerous."

"I don't care!"

Deacon froze, then turned in exasperation.

"Did you hear me?" Deacon shouted. "I said, no!"

Thomas, shocked by Deacon's harsh treatment, responded with an almost-whisper: "Deacon... please."

Deacon knelt. Taking Thomas by the shoulders, he spoke softly to the boy.

"Thomas, do you know what's going on here? We are only one step ahead of Darcon... if he..."

Deacon struggled for words, then: "People are dying. People just like Loren and Ellie. Don't be fooled by this feast, boy. These people are clinging to hope, yes, but amid great oppression. We are determined to hold to joy, despite our mighty suffering and many losses. There is hope. But we can't go in there now. We can't risk it, the timing is not yet right. Thomas, do you understand?"

Thomas glared at the ground, then wrenched away in hurt and anger.

"I understand. I understand you don't care if I ever find my dad. You don't care if we never get home!" he spat, then turned and fled into the darkness.

"Thomas!" Deacon called after him helplessly.

Chapter 54

The full moon glowed in the night sky, illuminating a lone sentry, sitting in his brown dragon's saddle and perched high on a cliff. He was on the far outer edge of the Home's boundary. He felt a little sorry for himself as he remembered this was the night of the big feast.

The rider scanned the horizon then stopped and squinted at a single point in the distance. There was a darkness on the horizon. It looked like a thunderstorm brewing, but not quite. Something was not right. The darkness grew.

"Shadow warriors!"

He put his battle horn to his lips. But before he could sound the warning blast, a black arrow pierced his chest, and he tumbled over the cliff and into the chasm of darkness.

Chapter 55

"Dad, where are you? I want to go home." Thomas moaned into the pile of hay where he lay. After he left Deacon, he had just run. Where? He had no idea. He ran till he was exhausted, and his tired legs would carry him no longer.

He had heard the familiar growl of a dragon and, following it, had made his way to this hewn-out rock stable in the dragon hold. There he had found his giant friend, Thorn.

Thorn sensed Thomas's anguish. He extended his long neck and gently nuzzled the boy with his nose.

Thomas rolled over. "Hey, Thorn."

Thorn rumbled in response.

"Sorry, I flunked dragonese."

Thorn grunted.

"Thanks for the effort."

"Thomas?" A female voice called from the darkness.

Thomas turned to see Ellie.

"I saw you leave the feast. You're not having fun?"

"No," Thomas hesitated. "No, it's not that... It's just, I

miss my dad, and I want to go home. But I can't go back without my dad. And if I can't find him, then I'm stuck... I'm not even sure how I got here, really."

Ellie sat beside Thomas in the hay.

"There's a reason Deacon won't take you."

"Yeah, he just keeps telling me it's dangerous. Darcon, Schmarkon! I'm not afraid of him! Why I—"

"You should be afraid!" Ellie leaned in to cut Thomas off. "Darcon's troops killed three of my brothers, and took Deacon's..." She paused, unsure of saying more, then forged ahead: "Deacon lost his wife and son. They were all killed by Darcon... Thomas, he can't let that happen to you."

Chapter 56

John plopped two mugs of ale down on the table in front of a melancholy Deacon, then sat in the chair beside him. "You look like you could use this."

"Thanks," Deacon responded half-heartedly.

"What's with the doom and gloom, man?"

"Thomas doesn't understand what's going on here. He hates me for not taking him to his father."

"So why don't you help him understand?"

"How?"

John frowned at Deacon. "Well, for starters, you could admit your real motives for not taking him."

"What's that supposed to mean?" Deacon growled.

"Come on, brother. The riding jacket Thomas wears looks strangely like the one you gave Aiden."

Deacon stared at John, then responded flatly: "I know Thomas is not my son."

"But the same thing could happen to him..."

Deacon's head dropped.

"You won't take him to his father because you can't bear the loss."

All the loss, all the hurt, welled up in Deacon as the scar was reopened.

"I failed. I was not there for my family when they needed me most." Deacon stared into his ale. "How do I deal with that?"

John knew the pain all too well.

"You're asking me?" And with tears leaking, he reached over and pulled Deacon into an embrace, as the two macho men shared the agony of losing both their families.

After just a moment, though, the two soldiers pulled apart and self-consciously wiped their eyes.

Changing the subject, John looked to the sky. "Looks like a storm is coming."

A dark cloud moved across the full moon, eclipsing it for a moment.

Deacon followed John's gaze. "That's no storm," he said ominously, as giant winged beasts swarmed out of the cloud.

Chapter 57

A battle horn echoed through the canyon. Everyone froze. Dancers stopped dancing. Feasters stopped eating. Children ceased running.

A moment of silence, as the community collectively held its breath, all asking themselves the same question: Was that what I thought it was? Then all the questions were answered as the horn blasted again, and the valley erupted into mayhem.

Mothers grabbed their children, and men shared hurried embraces with their wives, then rushed to their dragons.

―――――

The horn blast reached the stable. Ellie sprung to her feet in an instant.

Confused, Thomas rose slowly from the hay.

"What's wrong?"

"They've found us," she responded gravely.

———

Chaos filled the canyon floor. Deacon and John ran into its midst, shouting as they went: "Riders, to your dragons! The rest, to the stronghold!"

A woman fell in front of Deacon. He deftly helped her up, and she gained confidence from his steady hand. Then she ran on her way.

Deacon looked to the sky and called loudly: "Thorn!"

Chapter 58

Lightning lit up the dark sky, revealing the magnitude of the shadow-warrior army. They came riding on the storm —their hideous beasts in tight formation, the beat of their wings rumbled like a continuous roll of thunder.

One shadow warrior rode point: General Nawg. His iron breastplate glinted in the night, and his black cloak whipped behind him. From the back of his black dragon, he surveyed the terrified villagers scurrying far below him.

"Mine," he hissed.

Nawg spurred on his beast, and they dove followed by the black wave of shadow warriors.

Chapter 59

Thorn leaped from the cliff and into the sky, trumpeting his battle cry.

Running out of the stable, Ellie and Thomas watched Thorn take to the air.

"Go, Thorn, go!" Thomas hollered.

"Come on!" Ellie yelled to Thomas as she ran off at full speed.

"Wait up!" Thomas called, trying to catch up with her. Then she had a thought, and, looking over her shoulder, she let out a whistle and yelled: "Splinter!"

Within the stable, a small emerald dragon jumped to attention, then took herself into the air to catch up with Ellie.

Thomas felt Splinter fly over him, then was amazed as Splinter passed Ellie and flew out of sight over the upcoming cliff. Thomas was even more amazed when Ellie sprinted straight to the edge of that cliff... and leaped off it.

Thomas screamed—"Ellie!"—Then skidded to a stop

on the cliff's brink… in plenty of time to see Ellie land securely on the well-trained Splinter's saddle.

"Wow," Thomas breathed in awe. Then he shifted his gaze to the further-out cliffs overlooking the valley, and deep dread filled him.

Shadow warriors and their dark steeds streamed over those cliffs like a black waterfall, then plunged toward the valley below. Thomas cringed as, one by one, villagers were snatched from the ground by the dark dragons' ebony talons, or were cut down by a deadly rain of black arrows.

On the valley floor, a confused girl-child stood crying amidst the mayhem. The child was scooped up by the running John, who gripped his sword in one hand while handing the girl off to her frantic mother.

Just then—thunk!—a shadow warrior's heavy iron-tipped spear pierced into the ground just inches from John's toes.

John followed the spear's reverse trajectory, saw that shadow warrior bearing down on him. Like a madman, John broke into a sprint toward the beast and its rider.

Yet before they got down to John's level, he leaped atop one of the lined-up feasting tables, ran the length of two tables, then jumped high into the air just as the beast dove to attack. Which was to John's advantage, because he jumped clear over the beast's wing while also swinging his sword, and thus cleanly lopped off the shadow warrior's head.

The head fell one way and the body the other, then the riderless dragon squawked, wheeled, and turned back to the sky.

Chapter 60

Deacon ran through the chaos. As he stooped to assist another mother with her child, a shadow warrior leaped from his low-flying beast and knocked Deacon to the ground.

Deacon rolled over, just in time to block the thrust of the shadow warrior's jagged blade. Yet the warrior was larger than Deacon and had his full weight clamping Deacon to the ground.

The dark warrior raised his arm for another stab, but Deacon grabbed his wrist and stopped the knife's deadly trajectory. So the warrior bore down on that arm, inching the blade ever closer to Deacon's chest.

Deacon's veins popped, and beads of sweat rolled off his forehead as he tried to resist, his imminent demise seemed inevitable.

The jagged blade's sharp point began to dig into the leather of Deacon's jacket. Deacon thought: *Why keep resisting? Why continue this fight? Maybe it's time to join Aiden and my wife.*

Just then, the hulking shadow warrior was lifted, as

giant talons closed on him and ripped the screaming warrior off of Deacon and almost straight into the air.

Even better, the shadow warrior had barely begun his shadow-turn when Thorn's two vice-like talons simply pulled the warrior's neck from his body, then dropped the two lifeless clumps next to the remains of John's last opponent.

Then Thorn roared his victory, and Deacon had to acknowledge, even as he painfully stood: "Show off!"

Chapter 61

Thomas watched the battle from high above the canyon floor, just outside the cliff stable's door. He sighed as Ellie's red mane whipped in the wind, and she and Splinter dove to the battle.

"Let's go, girl!" Ellie encouraged her small dragon. Then Ellie pulled her sword from the saddle sheath, and Thomas saw the blade glint in the moonlight as she lifted it high, then aimed it at a flying-away shadow warrior.

Sensing Ellie's approach, that shadow warrior turned in his saddle, then quickly spurred his beast and steered it up to Ellie and Splinter's level. The smaller emerald dragon banked and bugled a surprisingly resonant challenge cry.

The shadow warrior hefted his heavy spear, took aim, and launched it. Ellie ducked in time, as the spear whistled past her ear.

———

On the ground, Deacon desperately fought several shadow

warriors at once, moving quickly to use their confusing numbers against them. But they managed to cooperate in semi-circling him up against a villager's house's wall, then one struck a tremendous counter-blow against Deacon's parry. This blow flung Deacon's sword out of his hand, and the blade flew end-over-end into the night.

Deacon watched briefly as his blade disappeared in the darkness, then swallowed and turned back to face what he thought was surely his death.

Yet the five shadow warriors did not stab at him. Instead, they all kept their swords aimed at his throat and gradually closed in on their prey while hissing like pit vipers.

Above, Ellie and Splinter dove to meet the spear-throwing shadow warrior, who had now drawn his sword. But the warrior's lumbering beast was no match for the smaller dragon's lightness and agility. When the shadow warrior swung his sword, Splinter evaded to the left, while Ellie's sword sliced off the warrior's sword arm.

The shadow warrior's arm fell, its hand still clutching the sword landing at Deacon's feet with a thud, sending up a puff of dust and startling the closing-in shadow warriors.

The dragon rider stared in disbelief for one millisecond, then snatched up the sword and cut the nearest shadow warrior in half before impaling the unfortunate warrior right next to him. Now the remaining three sensed that perhaps the tide had turned.

Chapter 62

High above the valley floor, perched on the threshold of the cliff-side stable, Thomas, now alone, watched the battle below in fear. Fires had sprung up here and there as shadow warriors stormed through the once peaceful village. Even from this distance, the piercing screams of dying people reached his ears. Finally, he tore his eyes from the chaos and ran, as fast as his legs could carry him, away from the horrific scene.

He had no idea where he was running—just away. Coming to the stairs cut into the cliff's side, he began climbing.

———

Astride his dark beast, one shadow warrior was making wide loops above the battlefield. He spied the odd-looking boy scurrying up the side of the cliff above the dragon stable. The warrior's spine stiffened: *Is this perhaps the Other-lander that Darcon and Nawg so desire?*

Red eyes blazing with ambition, the warrior spurred his beast into a sharp dive, right at the fleeing boy—Thomas.

From atop Splinter, Ellie saw the black dragon diving toward some prey. She leaned over her saddle and peered into the distance. She suddenly realized the beast's intent.

"Thomas!" she whispered, then ordered: "On, Splinter!"

Thomas scurried up the stone stairs, oblivious to the impending danger.

Licking his lips, the dragon-riding shadow warrior streaked toward his clueless, helpless prey.

Ellie bent low in the saddle and urged Splinter on. The sky's cold mist stung her face as she sped to the rescue.

The shadow warrior was almost on Thomas. The black dragon, fearsome talons flexed in anticipation, let out its blood-curdling screech and Thomas spun.

Horrified, the boy threw up his hands and closed his eyes, paralyzed like a tiny rabbit before a raptor.

Chapter 63

Another dragon's distinctive trumpet reached Thomas's ears. The boy's eyes popped open—"Splinter!"—And just then, the emerald dragon smashed into the black beast and sank her talons into its wing-flesh, forcing the creature out of the air and onto the stable's threshold. Thomas quickly back-pedaled up the stairs behind him. "Yeah! Get 'em, Splinter!" He cheered.

Despite the larger beast thrashing and swinging its tail to strike at Splinter or Ellie, the little dragon would not let go, and Ellie's swinging sword made several deep gashes in the black dragon's hide.

Meanwhile, the shadow warrior tried to figure out how to injure Splinter, to get his beast away, or to get out of his saddle and run across his dragon's talon-gripped wing to attack Ellie directly. He couldn't decide, for he didn't want to abandon the dragon he had worked so hard to own.

Just then, Ellie saw Thomas, frozen indecisively above her on the cliff stairway. She knew he was torn between fear for his life and concern for her, his friend.

Their eyes locked, and she commanded: "Run! Thomas! Run!" But he didn't.

Just then the shadow beast threw its head back to bite at Splinter, but the little dragon swiftly dodged those fangs —and, seeing an opportunity, just as quickly sunk her own sharp teeth into the other dragon's exposed throat, while still maintaining a tight grip on its injured wing.

Now screeching in pain, the beast thrashed and shook and flailed with wing and tail, but to no avail, it could not dislodge the little dragon.

Swinging his blade, the shadow warrior nicked Ellie's shoulder. Yet she continued to keep slicing and stabbing at the black dragon's side, even though her face was now locked in a pained grimace. And the shadow warrior seemed to be secured to his prized dragon.

Splinter forced the dark dragon toward the edge of the cliff in front of the stable. The bigger dragon could not find a foothold on the rock and steady itself, no matter how it scrambled.

That was because its loss of blood was beginning to tell. The flapping of its wings began to slow, its tail hung, and its neck jerks were weaker.

Splinter kept biting its neck deeper and deeper, and Ellie kept stabbing and slicing, and the shadow warrior considered and reconsidered his options, and the wounded dragon's belly poured out more and more black, oily blood.

Next, Splinter beat her wings with all her might, forcing the spent dragon backward over the cliff's edge. Yet the determined beast managed with the last breath to snag one talon around Splinter's saddle-belt.

So as the dying dragon's full weight slipped over the edge, Ellie and Splinter were dragged right over the precipice with it.

"Ellie!" Thomas shouted.

Ellie, realizing her fate, peered up one last time to see Thomas staring helplessly from the cliff.

"Go!" she commanded.

They fell.

"Noooo!" Thomas screamed in anguish.

The dark beast plummeted upside down, its wings akimbo as Ellie attempted to cut loose Splinter's harness so the black dragon's talon would dislodge. As the shadow warrior struggled for an escape, the ground rushed to meet them, and Splinter screamed.

Ellie cringed, preparing for impact. Both dragons smashed into the canyon floor with a bone-crunching thud.

The dust settled. The shadow warrior's black-gloved hand protruded from under his broken, dead beast.

Splinter was dazed but alive. The more massive dragon's body broke her fall, and Ellie didn't fall out of the saddle until after the impact.

Body aching, Ellie groaned and shook her head. As her eyes focused, she saw the twisted arm of her enemy. Relieved, Ellie reached up, stroked her little dragon's neck.

"Good girl, Splinter."

But Ellie's relief was short-lived. As she turned and struggled to stand, her rising eyes took in the black boots, dark cloak, and unmistakable steel breastplate of the looming General Nawg.

Chapter 64

Elsewhere on the valley floor, Deacon and John stood back to back, holding a horde of shadow warriors at bay. Thorn growled savagely as he stood his ground with them. Around them lay several bodies of those shadow warriors foolish enough to get within striking distance of either man's sword or the dragon's teeth.

In the sky, a new threat winged its way toward the men. Two shadow warriors, their dragons flying abreast, dragged between them a vast net of woven rope.

Both men, seeing their impending fate, broke and ran. Deacon yelled, "Thorn!" The great dragon turned to his master. "Thomas! Find Thomas!"

The mighty beast hesitated at Deacon's words, torn between loyalty to his master and obedience to his master's command. Thorn chose the latter. He coiled like a giant spring and launched into the sky—just before the net fell and knocked Deacon and John to the ground. The shadow warriors swarmed, covering the men like a colony of black bats.

———

Thomas ran along the top of the cliff. After he saw Ellie fall, he watched for a moment, hoping against hope that she and her little dragon would somehow be okay. Then he had finally followed his friend's command and ran.

As Thomas blindly rushed forward, he was surprised to realize he was longing to be sitting in his boring literature class back in Britain.

I would even gladly trade all this for a sorry game of cricket, Thomas thought. He missed Pudge. He missed his "mates." But more than anything, he missed his mom.

Even as he kept running, tears spilled from his eyes. He wondered what his mom was doing, and if she could ever forgive him for leaving.

Exhausted, Thomas slowed to a forced march. *If I could just find my father, he would know what to do. Dad would fix it all. He would know how to get us home, and everything would be right. We could be a family again.*

Thomas's thoughts were derailed by a thwapping sound that only a few days ago was utterly foreign to him; now, he recognized it as the beating of dragon wings in descending mode. *I knew it—they've finally got me!*

Ducking reflexively, Thomas looked back. He saw the dark silhouette of a colossal dragon swooping down on him from the night sky, blotting out stars as it loomed.

He tried to run, but tripped over a rock and fell, skinning his knee. Before he could scramble to his feet, massive talons reached out of the sky and snatched him. The ground dropped away as he screamed.

Then the beast carrying him trumpeted, and Thomas thought it was perhaps the sweetest sound he had ever heard.

"Thorn!"

Thomas relaxed as much as he could—given he was being held by the shoulders by a great dragon dangling him hundreds of feet off the ground.

"Thank you!"

Thorn trumpeted in response and beat his mighty wings quickly. They gained altitude and soared away from the stronghold.

"Good old Thorn," Thomas mused, as they sailed away from the battle and into the night.

Chapter 65

Quite some distance from the once-protected valley, a shadow warrior's beast glided slowly over tall jagged cliffs and impossibly smooth rock faces. Scanning but seeing naught, the warrior tugged his dragon's reins, and they began an adjacent circle, methodically searching many miles of hidden canyons and complex terrain.

Yet within the warrior's range, beneath the cliff edge, he had just surveyed, Thomas sat in the mouth of a good-sized cave, silently watching the dark scout from behind a pile of branches and brush that he had used to camouflage the cave's entrance.

As the beast turned and winged away, Thomas released a sigh of relief. Then he crawled to the back of the cave, where Thorn lay resting.

Thomas patted the huge dragon's head. "They're gone," he said bravely.

Thorn winced and whined softly—which confused Thomas. How could such a fierce, giant beast be in pain? Curious, Thomas looked the dragon up and down then exclaimed: "Thorn, you're hurt!"

Indeed, Thorn's hide was covered with wounds from the battle—scratches, bruises, and a particularly nasty gash across his neck. As Thomas gently moved to examine the gash, Thorn trembled and whimpered.

"I'm sorry, Thorn!... Wait, maybe there's something in your saddlebag."

Thomas moved to the bag and unbuckled its leather strap. He rummaged through the big saddlebag that only a few days back had been his airborne home.

"A-ha!" he exclaimed, finding a container of ointment. He scooped a dollop out, then gingerly approached the wounded dragon, showing him the blob all the way. Thorn sniffed the ointment and showed his disapproval with a low growl.

"Come on, boy," Thomas exhorted. "This is going to hurt me a lot more than it's going to hurt you." Holding an uninjured spot of Thorn's neck with one hand, Thomas started to use his other hand to apply the dollop to the wound.

But Thorn would have none of it. He pulled his head back in protest, so Thomas could no longer reach the gash. *This is going to be harder than I expected.*

Considering the stubborn dragon, Thomas had an idea. He walked two steps toward the cave opening, then yelled in surprise: "Shadow warrior!"

He pointed fiercely, and as he did, Thorn's head swung toward the opening—muscles taut, ready for action. But the dragon saw nothing, but the piles of brush still camouflaging the mouth of the cave… then howled in pain at the searing sting he felt as Thomas smeared the healing ointment along his wounded neck.

"There," Thomas said proudly. "All done." Thomas swaggered a bit as he wiped his hands on a rag. He then placed the ointment back in the saddlebag.

Thorn glared and growled at his small doctor, but Thomas wasn't intimidated. He returned the glare and shook his head at his colossal patient. "Big baby."

Chapter 66

Daniel Colson sat among the stacks of parchments and vellum books, scratching notes on the paper before him with his fountain pen. At least they had ink here. Suddenly his hand froze, and his eyes blinked in time with the screen's cursor. Then he whispered urgently, "What am I doing here?!"

His question echoed off the chamber's stone walls. Before the echo died, Daniel leaped to his feet and swept the notes off the table. Striding across the floor toward his high window, Daniel strained against his chain and gazed at his small slice of the heavens... the sky here was filled with different stars than Earth's —constellations for which he had no name. Where in the world was he? No. Correction. Where in the galaxy—maybe the universe?

His lust for knowledge had consumed him and led him to this place. Now aware, could he make it back? He had to! He had to make it home. But how?

Chapter 67

In Thomas's cave, a small fire crackled. Thomas threw another stick on the fire. Sparks flickered up to join the smoke that rose and spread across the rock roof.

Thomas crawled back beside his large reptilian companion, who still rested in the rear of the cave. Thomas examined Thorn's neck. Where the gash once oozed, a cloth bandage and ointment now covered it.

Satisfied, Thomas reclined against Thorn's side. The dragon circled his tail protectively around the boy, and the beast's rhythmic breathing lulled Thomas toward sleep.

As his eyes began to close, he peered through an opening in the brush that hid the cave's opening. He remembered how his dad had taught him all of Earth's constellations, but this dark sky was filled with stars and constellations for which he had no name.

"Dad," Thomas whispered, "Where are you? Let's go home." Then he drifted off into dreams of riding a giant dragon, both of them methodically searching for a lost loved one.

Chapter 68

Daniel tore his gaze from the alien constellations and turned back into the chamber. As he stepped back to his work table, a fortress sentry's herald rang through the courtyard.

"Riders approach!"

Daniel hesitated, then peered up through the open window. He could see through the small opening Shadow warriors were approaching in a dark cloud of beast and beating wings.

He watched in awe as he saw two riding side-by-side, with a large bundle slung between their dragons. What could they be transporting?

Then the bundle moved, and what Daniel imagined almost knocked him over. He continued staring at the dragon-suspended bundle as they flew past the window and out of sight.

Daniel stepped back. Leaning against the table, he pulled off his glasses and ran his fingers through his hair. What was that? What had they caught? Could it be an animal? No, he knew enough now to wonder not what but who they had captured and what would this poor soul's fate would be.

Chapter 69

"No... no...!" Thomas whispered in anguish as he scanned the valley floor below him. The sun, low in the sky, had trouble penetrating the smoke that hung in the air, from fires that still smoldered. Bodies lay in twisted heaps, like broken rag dolls. Nothing moved. A deathly stillness lay over the valley.

"Deacon! Ellie! Loren!" Thomas shouted as he brought Thorn in low for a landing. Seeing what he thought had once been Loren's dwelling, Thomas jumped to the ground before Thorn had even touched down. The boy ran to the ruins, calling out as he searched desperately: "Ellie? Loren? Deacon?"

He pushed through the debris and rushed through the destruction, pulling aside this and that broken or burned piece of furniture or wall.

"Loren? Please, somebody... somebody be left."

Nothing.

Finally, exhausted from the search, and scuffed and skinned from digging through piles of wreckage, Thomas hung his arms limply and made his way out of the deci-mated building.

It had been Loren's house, he was sure. He looked forlornly back one last time, then walked his return path to Thorn.

Thorn, sensing and understanding Thomas's despair, sat back on his haunches, raised his massive head to the sky, and let out a mournful howl.

Thomas wiped a tear off his cheek with the back of his shirtsleeve. And that's when he heard it—almost impercep-tible between Thorn's grieving howl: a low groan. He froze, listening. Thorn began his lament again.

"Shut up!"

The big dragon clamped his mouth shut mid-howl.

"Sorry, Thorn. I thought I heard something." Thomas strained to listen.

Again he heard the groan.

Thomas followed the sound through the smoldering wreckage, praying that someone was alive. He finally came to a huge table that was on its side right up against a remaining wall. "Loren?" The groan came in response, and Thomas hollered: "Thorn! Over here!"

Bending and straining, Thomas tried with all his might to right the massive table, yet the table barely rose six inches, and Thomas was about to drop it.

But just then, Thorn shoved his nose under its edge and rolled it upright to reveal… Loren. The elder of Home was semiconscious and in bad shape. There was a jagged ugly cut along the side of his head.

"Loren!" Thomas exclaimed as he rushed to cradle his old friend. "Oh, Loren."

The old man opened his eyes, straining to see. "Ellie?"

"No, it's me, Thomas. Thorn is with me. Loren, I can't find anybody… I don't know what happened. Ellie told me to run, and I just ran, and, and…" Thomas's voice cracked, and he buried his head in Loren's chest.

"I saw her fall!" Thomas sobbed.

"Shhh… Thomas, you could have done nothing for her."

"But I left her."

"There isn't time for that now. You must listen to me. If Darcon discovered this stronghold," Loren gasped, "he must know of the others."

"Others?" Thomas responded, again wiping his face on his sleeve.

"Yes, there are many of us." Loren struggled as he reached to touch Thomas's face. His eyes regained some of their brightness. "You must warn them."

Thomas pulled back. "I can't… I—"

"Thomas, you must!" Loren insisted, cutting off the boy's protest. "If they are not warned, what happened here will be repeated again and again… until Darcon's grip has squeezed the very life from our land."

"You can go with me!" Thomas pleaded pathetically. But even as the words left his mouth, his realization of Loren's injuries assured him there was no way.

"Thomas, I cannot." Shaking his head, the old man looked up at Thomas with love. "I have another journey to make."

"No! You can get better. I'll help you!"

Ignoring Thomas's protest, Loren reached into his tunic and pulled out a pendant that hung from his neck. He attempted to take it off but was too weak.

"Take it."

"I can't, Loren; it's yours."

"I won't be needing it. Take it, and remember us when you get home."

At the mention of his home, Thomas stilled. He gently

took the pendant off over Loren's head, looked at it a serious moment. Thomas recognized the symbol. The design he had seen so many times in his father's research. But this one had a dragon entwined with the circle.

"The symbol," Thomas whispered.

"Yes, the Creator's symbol."

Thomas then lifted it up and put it on. "Do you really think I'll ever get there, Loren?"

"I know you will." The old man nodded toward the pendant. "And this will help you find the way. There are ancient stories told of an Otherlander. One who would bear the pendant and drive the darkness from our land. He knows the secret of the pendant. It unlocks the Door through the mist and to Otherland, your world."

"Loren..."

"Thomas, enough. It is time for you to go... Thorn knows the way to the strongholds. He will take you. You must make the second stronghold before nightfall."

Thomas hesitated a moment, then embraced Loren for what he knew would be the last time.

"Go now, boy, and may the Creator strengthen you and guide your journey."

Agonized, Thomas found a charred board and used it as a makeshift pillow for Loren's head. Thomas stepped back, and Thorn shuffled in close to sadly lay his muzzle on his old friend's chest.

"Take good care of him, old boy," Loren said, stroking the dragon's nose.

As Thomas climbed into the saddle on Thorn's back, Loren gazed at them both with love, admiration, and concerned hope.

He knew he was sending a small boy on a warrior's mission, and the risks were high. But somehow, he felt confident, this was right.

"Walk the path of the Creator. Do not turn from it. Goodbye, Thomas."

One last time, Thomas looked down at his old friend. How could he leave him? Then, with a newfound resolve, he solemnly wiped a tear from his cheek, took a breath, set his face to the sky, and shouted: "Up, Thorn!"

The dragon hesitated a moment, then obeyed his young master. He leaped into the sky, took wing, and they flew off toward the darkening horizon.

Chapter 70

"We must have been flying for hours." The great Thorn was single-minded in his purpose, and flew a path known only to him. They landed only twice: once because Thorn sensed danger, and hid just in time so a flying shadow-warrior scout wouldn't see them, and once for Thomas to relieve himself.

Then, as the sun was just sinking behind the mountains, they crested a canyon wall and below them spread the second stronghold.

Thomas breathed a sigh of relief. "There it is, Thorn. Take us down."

Thorn bugled, and was answered by another dragon in the distance.

"Rider approaches!" shouted a sentry astride his dragon atop his rocky perch.

Thorn glided in for a landing as men ran to meet them. Thomas almost fell from the saddle in exhaustion, but strong arms steadied him.

And Thomas began talking as fast as he could: "The

shadow warriors are coming! Hurry, get ready! They attacked our stronghold last night—"

"Let a man through!" demanded Tuncan , the burly leader of the second stronghold. The men parted and allowed their leader access to the boy. He had a mass of black hair on his head and on his chin as well.

"We were having a feast," Thomas continued, almost delirious. "They came out of the clouds, and there was thunder and lightning, and all sorts…"

Tuncan interrupted with a rumble. "Hold on there. I know the beast Thorn, but you're a wee bit small to be his rider."

"I'm Thomas. Deacon and Ellie are my friends."

At the name of their General, a solemn hush fell over the men.

"Where is Deacon?"

"I don't know. Loren told me to warn you because—"

Tuncan silenced Thomas by laying his large hand on the boy's thin shoulder, and said patiently: "We understand, little man." Then Tuncan turned to his men and ordered: "Flint, prepare the men. Tal, ready the stronghold. Kalen, send riders to the other strongholds. Tell them it's time."

Chapter 71

Jingling keys and then screech of the lever alerted Daniel that the door to his cell was about to open. A moment of indecision, and then he stood, picked up his chair, and stepped toward the door as it swung open. Daniel lifted the chair above his head as someone stepped through. It was the servant girl. Daniel stopped mid-swing and set the chair on the floor.

The girl turned. She was holding a mug of water and a loaf of bread. As Daniel stepped forward, the girl caught his eye for a moment then quickly looked to the floor.

"Sir, I have brought you food and water."

"Thank you," He said as she took the food and sat it on the table.

The girl backed to the door, her head bowed to the floor submissively.

"Please, Miss, what is your name?" Daniel asked gently.

She stopped unsure of herself. Unaccustomed to receiving even the smallest act of kindness.

"Mia," She softly said to the floor.

"Mia, that's a nice name."

He stepped toward the door as she continued backing. Daniel intended to get the door for her, but he reached the end of his chain. Looking from his shackle to the girl. "Forgot," he said, shrugging his shoulders and lifting his chained ankle. "This is as far as I go."

The girl opened the door and began to step through, then paused long enough to whisper, "Thank you."

Chapter 72

"But the other strongholds!" Thomas protested as he was pushed into the living area of Tuncan's rustic home.

"It's taken care of, boy. You did a fine job. Now we have to take care of that dragon of yours and your stomach."

Tuncan marched Thomas to a rough-hewn table, forced him into the chair, and bellowed toward the home's kitchen: "Mollye!"

Tuncan's sturdy wife entered, carrying a massive plate of food. She placed it before Thomas, who immediately started eating, but also never stopped talking.

"I'm not hungry. Oh, mmm!... But what about Deacon? Wow, that's good!... And what if Ellie's still alive? Mmm!... I have to find my father, 'cause if Darcon has him, then..."

Tuncan looked to his wife with a smile. "Look after him."

"I will," Mollye said as she sent her husband off with a kiss. "You be careful, Tuncan."

With that said, she sat next to Thomas, who had finally given up talking and was now ravenously eating.

Mollye raised her eyebrows. "Not hungry, were we?"

———

Mollye was attempting to tuck Thomas in, but the adrenaline-pumped boy sat up in the bed yet again. Used to such, the motherly woman just pushed him back down, with an "I know, I know; you weren't hungry, and you're not sleepy either."

"I've got to find my dad," Thomas protested as he attempted to sit up again.

Mollye pushed him back down. And this time, she held him firmly but gently.

"You've had a big day. And yes, there is still much to be done. But tomorrow, because even a soldier needs his rest."

Thomas stifled a frowning yawn and struggled to keep his eyes open.

"But—but my dad..." The exhaustion finally won, and he drifted off to sleep.

Mollye leaned over and placed a little kiss on his forehead.

"Sleep well, little soldier."

Chapter 73

Daniel poured over his research. He felt he was getting closer, like on earth days before he cracked the code to Mairead Fhada and was able to open the door. But he was faced with a horrible decision. If he wanted to go home, then he must learn how to open the door. But if he opened the door, he would allow the evil of Darcon to slip through into his world. He prayed for wisdom and strength to make the right decision.

The familiar screech of the rusty door handle brought him out of his rumination. He looked out his high window and saw the moon in the night sky. It was the usual time now that Mia would bring his bread and water.

The door swung open, and his shy cowering friend stepped through. They actually had a few conversations over the last week. If you could call them that. He had learned that Mia was from a small village many miles from Darcon's fortress. Darcon's armies had swept over her land like a mighty tidal wave leaving a mass of destruction in its wake. They killed her father and brothers and took her, and her mother and sisters into slavery separating them. Mia had been serving here for many years.

Daniel was struck with the weight of her predicament, asking her if she ever thought she would be able to go home. He would never forget the look in her eyes as she said with resignation, "I will die here."

Mia stepped into his cell with his mug of water and bread. Her head was held customarily bowed with her eyes to the floor

"Good evening Mia, it's good to see you," Daniel said warmly.

The servant girl ignored his greeting and handed him his water and bread.

"How are you this evening?" Daniel attempted again to engage the young girl.

She stood stone still.

Daniel took a step toward her dragging his chain behind him.

"Is everything okay?"

Mia didn't respond but reached toward her face slowly. Her hand disappeared for a moment behind her dark hair that hung down. She glanced up toward the door, making sure that it was closed then bringing her hand to her mouth, she pursed out her lips and drew something from out of her mouth.

Mia grabbed Daniel's hands, pressing something small and hard into his palm. Then peered into his eyes and whispered, "For the Kingdom."

She whirled in a fluttering of robes and was out of the door, leaving him dumbstruck.

He dropped his gaze and slowly uncurled his fingers. There, like a symbol of hope, lay a wrought iron key.

Chapter 74

Mollye finished straightening up her humble living area. She stepped to the hearth where a large iron pot hung over the fire cooking. A spicy beef aroma wafted through the room as she lifted the lid and gave the stew a little taste. "Aye, that'll do the trick," she said pleased with her cooking. It was the greatest gift that the Creator had given her. And she put it to good use feeding anyone and everyone that came into Tuncan and her home.

If Thomas stayed with them for any length of time, she would put some real meat on his bones. "Poor little dear." He was still sleeping. Her motherly instincts kicked in. She should probably wake him and give him some of her lovely stew. He must have slept three hours, at least.

"Thomas?" Mollye knocked gently on the door of the bedroom, where Thomas slept. "Thomas, it is time to get up." Still no answer.

Mollye pushed the door open. "Everything is ready, we must—" She stopped mid-sentence.

The bed was empty. Thomas was gone.

Chapter 75

On the cold stone wall of Darcon's prison, a grinning skeleton hung by rusted steel manacles. Hanging next to that skeleton was another skeleton, then another. And hanging beside the final skeleton was Ellie, with manacles biting into her wrists.

She blew her red mane off her face and looked left, attempting to see Deacon.

"Do something, will you?"

Hanging next to Ellie, John also looked to his left.

"Pardon me... what was that?" Deacon responded sardonically; after all, he was in the same predicament as the rest.

"Can you do something?"

"I'm thinking!" Deacon responded.

"Well, think harder!"

Chapter 76

Mordis Saldan stepped into Daniel's dim, musty cell flanked by his two hulking prison guards.

"Professor, I've come to hear about your progress."

Daniel stood. "As I've told you for the last twenty-three days, I don't know how to get through the door. I'm working as hard as I can. I will let you know when I have the key."

"Professor, do you need more motivation?"

The two guards stepped forward, leering at him, wielding their truncheons.

Daniel locked eyes with Mordis. "Can't do your own dirty work, can you, Mordis? Always have to hide behind the skirts of Tweedledee and Tweedledum."

That got a reaction. A slight upturn at the corner of Mordis' mouth.

He spun to the guards.

"Leave us."

The guards paused but only for a moment and then retreated, closing the massive door behind them.

A glint sparked in Mordis's typically cold eyes, like a

predator considering his prey. He stepped forward, reaching into the fold of his dark cassock. His hand clutched his dagger.

Daniel stepped forward, straining against his chain tether.

Mordis smiled. He was going to enjoy this.

Daniel then shook his leg, and unbelievably the shackle released and dropped, with a clang to the stone floor.

Mordis stared in shock at Daniel's free ankle.

He looked up to see Daniel grinning and holding an iron key in front of his face. Then Daniel palmed the key, curled his fingers into a tight fist. Mordis took a breath to scream but instead received a solid punch right to the jaw. He slumped to the floor, unconscious. Outside the prison door, hearing the thump Tweedledee and Tweedledum shared a knowing glance. Their master enjoyed taking care of prisoners.

Inside his cell, Daniel tore a sleeve from his old shirt and gagged Mordis. He quickly stripped Mordis of his cassock and dressed him in his own soiled and threadbare clothing. He retrieved the dagger that Mordis always kept secreted within his robes and carefully shaved his own head with it nicking himself a few times.

Daniel unlocked the chain from the iron ring in the center of the floor and locked it instead on Mordis's ankle then pulled him to the wall.

He pushed the table against the wall under the window and unceremoniously flopped Mordis onto it. He grabbed his leather satchel that he had packed earlier and slung it over his shoulder.

Daniel then took the wooden chair and putting it on the table, used it to precariously reach the high window in the cell wall. He leaped and grabbed the edge and finding purchase, straining with all his might he pulled himself up into the window.

Once there, he finally surveyed the scene outside and below. He knew a fall from this height would surely kill him. On the ramparts around the castle wall, fires burned, and sentries kept their vigilant watch.

A trumpet sounded as a rider on a black beast winged toward the fortress. The sentries' attention was drawn toward the approaching rider. Below him, by many feet, Daniel could see a balcony down and to the left. This may be his only chance. He held to the shackle that once had been his imprisonment, which now would provide his freedom. He clutched tightly, said a prayer, and launched himself through the window. The twenty feet of chain quickly clanged through the stone window. Daniel fell till he stopped abruptly held by the anchor that was Mordis's body.

The sharp yank on Mordis's ankle sent a shock of pain through his body, and he came too, moaning as he hung upside down against the stone wall. He attempted to scream but was prevented by the gag.

Against the wall outside fifteen feet below, Daniel began to swing back and forth like a pendulum.

Inside and hanging by his ankle, Mordis worked his chin, attempting to dislodge the gag. Almost there.

Daniel swung again, at the top of his arc, released the chain dropping to the balcony below.

The released chain zipped back through the window link by link just as Mordis attempted to scream but instead he dropped with a crash to the stone floor and was knocked out cold, again.

Hearing the crash, outside the cell door, Tweedledee chuckled to Tweedledum. "The master's having fun today, eh."

Chapter 77

Daniel walked briskly with his head down, hoping to find a way out of the labyrinth of halls that made up Darcon's fortress.

His disguise of Mordis's black cassock, his shaved head, and twenty-five days of beard growth enabled him to make it this far. Twice he had passed guards standing at their post and mumbled a greeting without raising suspicion. As he turned a corner, he overheard two soldiers talking.

"Ragnon said for us to get to the courtyard on the double. The supply wagon will be arriving later tonight, and he wants us to relieve the guards there."

"Lazy mutts."

"Yeah, I said we would be there right away. I don't fancy another flogging."

"Nor do I!"

Daniel fell in behind the grumbling soldiers, and keeping his distance, followed them through the tunnels.

The torch-lit passages finally came to an opening, and before he knew it, Daniel had stepped into the courtyard. His breath was taken away just by being in the open air.

The sun was setting on the horizon. He quickly stepped back into the shadows of the tunnel to survey his surroundings. The courtyard was a large cobblestone square flanked on each side by high walls. Along the top of these fires burned with guards posted and wielding crossbows. Three hundred long feet away was the gate, which led to the outside. It was protected by a portcullis, a vertical sliding wooden grill shod with iron suspended in front of the gateway. If he made it across the courtyard without being shot, he still had to get through the gate, and the portcullis was shut tight.

Chapter 78

Daniel hid in the shadow of the tunnel that exited into the courtyard. He peered at the only way out a gate, three hundred feet away and blocked by an iron portcullis. And between him and the gate companies of human soldiers were preparing for war overseen by shadow warriors. Orders were being shouted. Weapons were being sharpened. The busy work of Darcon's war machine.

He had to make it. He hoped his disguise would work. Just then, a horn sounded, and the great wheel and chains that raised the iron portcullis turned and, groaning, began to recede into the wall above.

Daniel cast around, and seeing no better opportunity, said a prayer, and stepped from the protection of the shadows into the courtyard.

"You are Mordis Saldan." He told himself as he straightened and attempted to emulate Mordis's walk of authority. A sentry from the wall turned when he saw the movement. Daniel held his breath but kept moving. The sentry then recognized the black cassock and turned his back on the man and continued his surveillance of the outer perimeter.

Daniel allowed himself to breathe again.

Two hundred feet.

The portcullis continued to rise, and Daniel kept walking.

One hundred fifty feet.

It was all he could do not to make a dash for it.

One hundred feet

The portcullis continued to rise. He was almost there.

"Stop that man!" a voice rang through the courtyard.

Daniel froze and turning saw Mordis with his two guards stepping into the courtyard. But He was dressed in Daniel's tattered clothing, and his beard was cut off.

Daniel straightened and pointed at Mordis and shouted with as much bravado as he could muster, "Seize him!"

The guards on the walls hesitated. At this distance, they were not able to tell who was shouting the orders. They certainly wouldn't shoot the black-cassocked Mordis.

Daniel turned on his heels and marched swiftly toward the gate.

Fifty feet.

"Stop him!" The command went up again.

The rising gate ground to a halt. Then to Daniel's horror reversed and began lowering.

"I am Mordis Saldan! I command you to stop the prisoner."

The crossbow-wielding sentries now leveled their bows at Daniel, and he took off.

The portcullis was now steadily closing as he sprinted.

Twenty-five feet.

The iron spikes were almost to the ground. Daniel heard the multiple twangs of crossbows and felt the bolts whizz by. He listened to the pounding of boots behind him. He dove and rolled missing being impaled by the spikes as they slammed into the ground.

The Sentries loaded their crossbows for a second volley.

Daniel thrust onto his feet. He thought his heart would burst with the exertion. The forest was just ahead.

Almost there. Then the forest was obscured in a rush of wind, and a wall of shiny black scales as a shadow warrior astride his black beast landed directly in front of Daniel with its wings unfurled. It opened its gaping, fanged mouth and gave a piercing screech.

Daniel skidded to a halt covering his ears in agony. He fell to his knees and screamed his own frustration. The freedom of the forest taunted him just beyond the black beast.

Chapter 79

The sun was low. Sheer canyon walls the color of scarlet surrounded Thomas and Thorn. The sky above was a thin band of azure. The boy and his dragon took turns as they drank from a cold rushing stream.

"Man, that is good!" Thomas declared, flinging water droplets everywhere.

Thomas had slept soundly for a few hours after Mollye fed him and forced him to bed. But then his eyes had popped open, and all he could think about was finding his dad.

He had lain in that soft bed a few more minutes until he became fully conscious. He could hear Mollye humming to herself as she worked in the kitchen. His mom did that.

That was all it took. Thomas got dressed, scurried out the window, and was off to fetch Thorn and start looking again.

Suddenly, here in the canyon, Thorn rose up on his haunches, at full alert. His brilliant eyes searched the canyon walls, and a low growl emanated from deep within the wary dragon's chest.

Thomas, knowing now to trust his large friend's senses, froze. Like Thorn's, Thomas's eyes searched along the dark crevices in the cliffs' faces.

Nothing. Still, Thomas didn't dare breathe. Then a blood-curdling screech echoed through the canyon, and two shadow warriors on black beasts swooped over the canyon's rim and plummeted toward Thomas and Thorn.

Thomas bolted for Thorn, and the dragon launched into flight even as Thomas finished seating himself into the saddle. Thorn darted straight up in front of the darker beasts, and the chase was on!

Thorn punished the air flying faster and faster but to no avail. The dark riders were gaining.

Thomas searched the saddle for something, anything he could use against the gaining threat. There, Deacon's sword was still in its sheath, lashed to the seat.

Thomas bravely grabbed the sword's hilt and pulled. It didn't budge. Struggling with both hands, Thomas slowly drew the blade. As the sword's tip left the sheath, the full weight of all that iron pulled it right out of Thomas's grip. "Heads up!" he exclaimed forlornly, as he watched the sword fall through the trees.

Thorn jetted out of the canyon, the shadow warriors in tow. Thomas continued searching the saddlebags. He found an apple and launched it at his nearest pursuer.

"Go away!"

The apple smacked the first rider in the chest. Encouraged by this success, Thomas emptied the saddlebag, launching the contents one by one at his chasers.

Just then, Thorn folded back his wings and dove down into the canyon, streaking toward the floor. Thomas hung on for dear life.

The ground rushed to meet them. But before impact,

Thorn pulled up skimming the surface of the river along the canyon bottom. No good. The pursuers were still unshaken. It was like they were tethered to him.

Thorn flew along one of the canyon walls, his tail extended as usual when flying. The closest dark beast snapped but missed. As the creature lunged forward to try again, Thorn suddenly swung his mighty tail—slamming the zooming beast and its rider into the canyon's wall; they fell in a spinning heap.

"Yeah!" Thomas cheered, as he watched them tumble toward the river below.

Thomas looked back for the other shadow warrior, saw nothing. Then he turned forward and was shocked to see the warrior and his beast right beside them.

This dark soldier must have used Thomas and Thorn's distraction to fly unobserved into this lethal position.

The shadow warrior suddenly stood in his saddle, then reined his beast even closer. Its leathery wingtips almost brushed against Thorn's. *What is he doing?* Then Thomas understood. The warrior coiled like a spring, then—to Thomas's dismay—leaped!

Thomas cringed, bracing for the soldier's impact. But Thorn suddenly braked in mid-flight, and the outsmarted shadow warrior went flailing past them, smashed into the rock wall and careened to the ground, toward his death.

Thomas breathed a sigh of relief and patted his friend's golden neck. "You're the greatest, Thorn!" Thorn trumpeted in agreement.

Chapter 80

Daniel drifted in and out of consciousness. Through a veil of pain, he slowly came to. Where was he? Then Daniel remembered his attempt at escape. The forest was so close! Then the guards set upon him with their punches and kicks, and he had been knocked out. He had no idea how long it had been since the beating, but the wounds felt plenty fresh. He ached all over. He must be somewhere in the bowels of the earth below Darcon's fortress. He tried to sit up, but pain wracked across his torso. Probably have a broken rib or two. He finally managed with difficulty and attempted to take in his surroundings, which was impossible because it was pitch black. His glasses? Where were his spectacles? He moved his hand along the damp floor, searching for them and recoiled in terror as he felt something alive skitter across his fingers. Somewhere in the darkness, he heard a squeak and more rustling. Rats!

There, on the floor, he finally felt the metal frame. His hand closed on his spectacles. One lens was cracked!

Could it get any worse? The darkness, the pain, the loneliness suddenly it all washed over him in a sea of despair. He lay back on the cold, damp floor. He didn't care anymore. This is where it would end. He pushed his spectacles back on, and squinting up saw a tiny prick of light like a minuscule North Star. A tiny hole? A crack in the wall? Unbelievably that little point of brightness gave a lift to his spirit. *Even here, the darkness does not prevail.*

Daniel lay still as his mind searched, then he took a breath and began:

———

"The Lord is my shepherd; I shall not want.
He maketh me to lie down in green pastures:
He leadeth me beside the still waters.
He restoreth my soul:
He leadeth me in the paths of righteousness
for his name's sake.
Yea, though I walk through the valley of the shadow
of death,
I will fear no evil:
For Thou art with me;
Thy rod and Thy staff they comfort me.
Thou preparest a table before me in the presence of
mine enemies:
Thou anointest my head with oil; my cup runneth
over..."

Daniel choked, overcome with emotion. He couldn't go on. The silence bore down on him.

And then a voice spoke out of the darkness taking up the refrain:

"Surely goodness and mercy shall follow me all the
     days of my life:
and I will dwell in the house of the Lord forever."

Was he hallucinating? But then the voice spoke again from the darkness.

"Dr. Colson, it's been a long time."

Daniel recognized a distinctly British accent. His mind reeled. "Who are you?" He asked the darkness.

"I was saving this for a special occasion. I believe this will do," The voice said.

Daniel heard a sharp cracking on the stone floor and saw tiny sparks. Then one spark took hold, and he listened to the soft blow of breath, and a flame ignited, shedding light within the cell.

A shadow of a man sat huddled in the corner holding a rustic candle.

"Forgive me if I don't stand. I'm not the man I once was."

Daniel crawled toward the man. He was old and frail, dressed in rags. His hair was long and matted, and his face was covered by a long gray beard.

The man smiled. And his eyes lit up cheerily.

"It's about time. I thought you would never come."

Recognition slammed into Daniel's mind. "My Dear God, Albright, is it you?"

The man's smile brightened.

"Yes, Professor, nothing slips by you."

"But surely being here for only a month could not have had this effect on you?"

"A month?"

"Yes, Albright, I followed you through Mairead Fhada only by a few hours. Today is my twenty-sixth day here, by my reckoning."

Albright nodded.

"I have been wondering if the door that opened to another 'where' might spin you off into another 'when.'" Albright scratched his beard.

It was all so disconcerting. Daniel could see the eyes and the smile of his young assistant, but the rest had his mind on tilt. He was almost afraid to ask but then swallowed and gave voice to his question, "How long have you been here?"

Albright sat very still, counting. "Thirteen, no, fourteen years," he whispered through cracked lips. "Yes, fourteen long years."

"But how?"

"I have had a long time to think about many things, the door, certainly being one of them."

Daniel interrupted. "If I came through the door, let's say two hours after you and you have been here 14 years, does that mean every hour in our universe is 7 years here?"

Albright nodded. "I can hear the paper that you will read before the Archeological Society, "The Dog Year Universe."

At this, both men chuckled.

Albright's laugh trailed off into a wheeze.

Daniel leaned forward with concern.

"I'm all right, doctor." Albright recovered. "What I wouldn't give for a spot of tea right now."

"Earl Grey?" The American asked.

"Of course."

"With a splash of milk?"

"The sine qua non of tea," said Albright.

"Yes, without milk, it's not tea."

The two prisoners sat quietly for a moment.

Then Daniel broke the silence. "I'm realizing that I

was thinking of our universes as being symmetrical. Fixed. "

"Go on."

"Our own planet moves along its orbit in our solar system. And our solar system moves in our galaxy. Our galaxy moves within the universe. It stands to reason that wherever this planet is, it must also be within its own solar system and galaxy and universe. To really understand how time works between the two universes, one would have to know the position of both relative to each other."

"Yes, I see where you're going," Albright said. "But if the universe is all that exists. Then this planet is somewhere within our universe. Unless, of course, we're dealing with a parallel universe."

Daniel nodded in the flickering candlelight. "About that, If our universe is parallel to N'albion's universe, then it might be like parallel streets running alongside each other. But to cross over from one street to the other, you would need a path to get there, a perpendicular street."

"Yes, and the stone circle is the perpendicular: the path from Earth to N'albion."

"Exactly. But the streets may be moving at separate speeds more like parallel train tracks with the trains moving at faster or slower speeds. If you jumped from one train car on one track to the other, you would land in a different numbered car depending on the relative speed and direction of the trains."

Albright settled back and gave another little cough.

Daniel could see the man was getting tired. He sighed, "We can hypothesize all night about this, err, it is night isn't it?

"Yes," Albright said.

"Well, we may never fully know."

"After fourteen years in this hole, I do know something."

"What is that?" Daniel asked.

"Though I walk through the valley of the shadow of death, I will fear no evil: for He is with me."

Chapter 81

Daniel considered the aged man that sat before him. The man that had been his young, robust, handsome assistant only a few short weeks ago. Reduced to this through the tortures of years under the cruel hand of Darcon and the likes of Mordis.

"Albright, I never knew you to be a religious man."

"I wasn't, and I'm not sure I am now." He sighed. "As I said before, I've had plenty of time to think about many things." Albright paused as if he was unsure if he should go on. "One of the first realizations was that I had wronged you."

Daniel was taken aback. "Albright?"

"No, Dr. Colson, please let me finish. I stole your research. Like a common thief. At first, I rationalized it: How I worked so hard for you, all the late nights. In my mind, it was my research. But that was a lie. You did the work, and it was brilliant," Albright smiled. "And that is where I realized I had gone wrong. I hated you for your brilliance. My pride would not allow me to see it."

Albright continued. "What God did here in this

dungeon was gracious. He showed me that there was someplace darker than this prison cell." Albright looked at Daniel. "My heart."

Daniel didn't know what to say. The old-young man continued.

"Dr. Colson, please forgive me. Forgive me for hating you, forgive me for stealing from you and causing you this horrible mess."

Immediately, Daniel responded, "My Dear Albright, of course, but it is I that need your forgiveness. I treated you as a servant or, worse, a slave and not as the talented colleague you deserved. It was my pride that caused me to chase after you. Blind to the damage it would cause my family or anyone else. I was reckless and stupid. Please forgive me."

Daniel reached and grasped Albright's hand, and they shook.

"Now, let's put our heads together and find a way out of here," Daniel said with a gleam in his eye.

Chapter 82

In the dim light of the dungeon cell, Albright smiled. "I have only one thing to say about your idea of escape… Rats!"

"Rats?"

"Yes, Dr. Colson. Rats." Albright held his makeshift candle aloft, filling the cell with its flickering, pale yellow light. "Look around, Doctor. The walls are stone. The floor is stone. The door is solid timber. Yet we are surrounded by our furry friends." Albright thrust his candle's flame toward the nearest rodent. It squeaked in pain and scurried away, its tail a little singed.

Daniel wasn't impressed. "So, we share the cell with vermin…"

"Shh," Albright hushed Daniel. "Watch."

He pointed toward the singed rat as it skittered to the far wall and made its way along until the rodent came to the corner and then with a squirm disappeared.

Albright smiled. "For months, I wondered how I could be sealed in a closed cell but still accompanied by a host of rats. Where could they get in? I began watching them carefully and sure enough finally found their ingress and egress."

The men scooted to the corner where the rat had performed its disappearing act.

Daniel examined the area and for the first time, realized the floor was paved with large flagstones. He searched and found a small hole at the corner of one large stone impossible to detect without the aid of the candle's light.

"Place your fingers in there, Dr. Colson."

"Seriously?"

"Trust me."

Daniel warily reached in nervous about receiving a rat bite. He was able to get only two fingers into the hole.

"Now, pull!"

Daniel gave a little tug.

"Pull, doctor!"

Daniel strained and felt the stone give way, unseated from its place.

Albright reached and grabbed the flagstone and lifted. The stone scraped up and fell over with a resounding thud that sounded like a bass drum.

Daniel flinched.

"Don't worry, Dr. Colson, the guards never come no matter the racket I make." Albright motioned. "Look."

Where the flagstone had once been was a hole almost two feet in ragged diameter. Daniel peered into the black hole. It was impossible to see a thing.

"Listen," Albright said.

Daniel stilled himself and turned his ear to the gaping hole.

The distinct sound of rushing water reached him from somewhere far below.

"A river?"

"Yes. It flows out of the mountain. The fortress is built

over it. The fortress retrieves fresh water from there, and it is the sewer as well. Before I was thrown in here, I saw where exited from under the mountain and flows into the forest."

"Sounds like a long way down."

A rat peeked its head over the edge of the hole, and before it could climb onto the floor, Albright gave it a swift kick, and the rat dropped with a squeak into the black abyss.

Daniel and Albright stared at each other listening. Then finally, they heard a faint splash.

"It is a long way down."

Chapter 83

The moon hung low in the night sky. Thomas and Thorn had flown through the day and into the night. Thomas leaned over in the saddle, to gaze down at the dark forest that stretched below them for miles. Solid but for the dark river that curved through it like a giant black snake.

"That's where you found me; isn't it, Thorn? I remember crossing that river."

Thorn growled in answer.

"Then we must be close. We better be careful."

Thomas squinted into the distance and could barely make out a glow at the far edge of the forest. "That could be firelight. Take us down, boy."

Thomas hung on tight as Thorn dove and glided down to the forest. He skimmed silently along the treetops until he found a small clearing to land in.

Thorn's head swung from side to side, his bright eyes searching for any hidden dangers in the surrounding underbrush.

Thorn growled.

"It's okay, boy," Thomas spoke as he slid from the

saddle. They had been in the air so long, walking on the firm earth seemed strange to his feet.

Thomas peered into the forest, then spoke to Thorn over his shoulder: "I'll have to walk from here. But I don't think it's that far."

Turning, Thomas took the dragon's triangular head in his hands and looked into his big friend's solemn eyes. "I want you to stay here."

Thorn rumbled his disapproval.

"No, you'll just slow me down." The small boy squared off with the huge dragon. "You're not made for walking, and you're too big to get through those trees. Besides, I need you rested and ready to fly when I come back with my dad."

Thomas gave Thorn's large head a pat, then turned and moved toward the trees. Thorn shuffled after him.

"No."

The dragon stopped.

Thomas began again.

Thorn followed.

Thomas stopped and glared firmly at the dragon. "Thorn, I said no!"

The dragon stopped.

"Sit!"

The colossal dragon plopped on his haunches.

"Stay!" Thomas ordered, staring down his big friend even as he backed toward the edge of the forest. "Good dragon." With that, he turned and stepped into the shadows.

He was instantly swallowed up by the forest, and Thorn was left sitting alone, whimpering.

Chapter 84

In the dungeon, Daniel sat back considering the hole that had been revealed after dislodging the large flagstone and the dark drop to the river far below. "Even if we were able to get out of here, we still don't know how to open the stone circle. We have to find the right constellation."

"Yes," Albright said, "We know the door may be opened by the combination of astrological time and walking the correct pattern within the stone circle. A timed combination lock if you will." Albright's eyes regained some of their old spark. "But there is another way. Doors can also be opened with keys."

"I'm listening."

"When I came through the portal, I was taken captive and like you forced to work on the solution to open the door. In my research, I came upon an ancient text with this verse:

Albright looked as if he were reading from a page that wasn't there as he pulled it from his memory:

"When the veil is thin
and the Warrior is armed
walk the path of the Creator
But be warned
Destruction awaits he
Who steps to the right or left."

A rat rustled somewhere in the darkness.

Daniel reflected on the verse, then said, "We know the 'veil being thin' is the time of Samhain or October in our world. Celtic lore speaks of a thinning of the wall that separates worlds during that season." And the 'path of the Creator' is the pattern that must be walked: The Celtic Trinity Knott."

Albright agreed, "Yes, yes, and we know that to open the door of Mairead Fhada in our world, the constellation Orion must be positioned low in the October sky."

"So, the 'armed warrior' is Orion, the Archer," Daniel said.

"Yes, but this world does not have the constellation, Orion. I believe there is another way for the Warrior to be armed." Albright leaned forward, a smile spread across his face like the Cheshire cat. "A key."

"A key?"

Albright reached into the folds of his threadbare shirt and retrieved a folded parchment. He continued as he unfolded it on the stone floor. "I came across this in my searching in the early days of my arrival."

Daniel illuminated the parchment with the candle to reveal a drawing of the Trinity Knott intertwined with a dragon crafted into a circular pendant.

The pendant that now hung by a gold chain from the neck of Thomas.

Chapter 85

Albright and Daniel replaced the flagstone. Then Albright, exhausted, lay back right where they were sitting, wished Daniel a goodnight was snoring within seconds. Daniel listened to the rats scratching somewhere in the darkness. Every time he tried to get comfortable on the cold stones, pain from his recent beating would shoot through his side. Besides that, his mind was spinning. Finding his young assistant in his present condition was inconceivable. But he was here, and he couldn't deny the facts before him. His young-old assistant. Now what? Another prison break? What else could he do? He had to get out of this hole and take Albright with him. He pondered the existence of another way to get through the door that was the stone circle and back home. In all his research on earth, he had never come across the reference to a key. This strange pendant engraved with the symbol of the Trinity and a dragon. How would they find this key? Well, first things first. Get out of this hole with Albright alive. Then home. Oh, to see his Caroline and Thomas again. Would they ever be able to forgive him? If Albright could, then perhaps his wife and son could too.

Chapter 86

"Dr. Colson. Wake up," Albright urgently whispered.

Still disoriented, Daniel attempted to focus on the person leaning over him.

"Albright?" Daniel cast about the dim cell lit only by Albright's candle. "Is it morning?"

"No, but I am afraid that we need to make our move now. I've heard a lot of movement and voices in the halls. Something is afoot, and it is best we don't wait around to find out what it is."

Daniel sat up with a grimace. His ribs still ached. "Are you sure?"

"No, I am not sure. If by sure you mean psychological confidence, but now is as good a time as any."

Daniel couldn't think of any good reason to disagree with Albright. And he didn't like the idea of sleeping in this rat infested hole another night.

The men moved to the flagstone. Daniel heaved it up, but this time carefully set it on the floor so as not to make a sound. Albright reached into the black hole that had been covered by the stone and retrieved a coil of rope. Daniel stared dumbfounded. "Where did you get the rope?"

Albright pointed to his head of matted hair. "You don't think I grow it like this for style, do you? Fourteen years of hair growth weaves into a pretty sturdy rope. I doubt it's long enough, but it will have to do."

Albright secured the end of the rope around a jut of rock inside the inner edge of the hole then handed the line to Daniel. "I think you should go first."

Daniel hesitated, then took the rope and shimmied through the small hole. It was precarious work as he slid down and felt his feet dangling in space. "I don't know. Are you sure about this?"

The all too familiar sound of keys jiggling and the creak of the obstinate lock stopped his question.

"Go, Dr. Colson! Now!"

"Albright!"

The timber door swung open with a groan.

"No time for discussion!" Albright shouted.

Two guards stepped into the cell closely followed by Mordis Saldan. They lifted torches high, flooding the room with light. There was a shout from Mordis. Albright pushed Daniel through the hole.

"No, I won't go without you," Daniel protested.

"Godspeed, my friend," Albright whispered.

And with a final shove, Daniel fell into the abyss.

The rope burned through his hands, only slowing his fall by degrees. He looked up one last time to see Albright peering down silhouetted by torchlight, and then he smacked into the ice-cold water of the underground river.

He plunged down into its depths, finally striking his back on the rocky bed. Daniel thrust off the bottom and shot toward the surface. He felt his lungs would burst, and then he surfaced sputtering and gagging carried along by the swift choppy current of the river.

"Albright!" Daniel shouted through the whitecaps of the river, then another wave smacked him in the face filling his mouth with water.

He couldn't be sure, but he thought he heard a shout and a splash. The swift current carried him along, and he couldn't worry about Albright now he had to focus on not drowning.

Soon, ahead of him, he could see light. The mouth of the cave. The river carried him along closer and closer to the mouth. Daniel could now make out huge stalactites and stalagmites in the cave. At one point, his thrashing awakened a colony of bats that burst from their resting place and swarmed over his head toward the cave opening.

Even though he still struggled to keep his head above water bobbing like a tiny cork in the raging current, Daniel was heartened by the growing light as the mouth of the cave approached.

The sound of the current was changing, though. Daniel was sure the roar of the river was getting louder. He peered ahead and realized too late why the river now made a deafening roar. Waterfall!

Daniel tried for the edge of the river to no avail. The current was too strong, and he was already there. Daniel could see the mist thrown up from the crashing water. One moment he plunged into it, then he was shot out into the moist air and fell along the path of the crashing river.

Daniel had the sense this time to take a massive gulp of air before hitting the pool at the base of the waterfall. He tumbled end over end underwater like a rag in a washing machine. Then mercifully, the undertow spit him out, and Daniel surfaced and swam to the rocky shore. Barely able to lift his limbs, he collapsed.

Daniel finally lifted his weary head. Albright! The professor crawled to his feet and peered up the waterfall. "Albright!" He attempted to shout over the roar of the waterfall. Then he saw Albright shoot over the waterfall into space and fall arms and legs all akimbo. The old man hit with a smack and sunk into the churning foam at the base of the waterfall.

Still exhausted, Daniel dove in and with a few labored strokes came to the center of the pool. Albright surfaced facedown in the water. Daniel grabbed him and drug him to shore.

Albright was unconscious. Daniel rolled him onto his side.

"No! Albright! Come back to me." Daniel started CPR. Between breaths praying, "Dear God, let him live."

Another breath and then Albright spit out a massive amount of water and with a raspy suck filled his lungs with air.

"Thank God!" Daniel laughed.

The frail Albright opened his eyes, and seeing Daniel gave a weak smile.

"Dr. Colson, Let's not do that again,"the old man muttered.

Daniel smiled and then froze as he heard the crunch of boots on gravel behind him.

He turned but not before the pommel of a sword cracked the back of his head, and he pitched forward onto his friend unconscious.

Chapter 87

Deacon slowly woke from a disturbing dream that his shoulders were on fire. Flames were shooting from his rotator cuffs. He raised his head and shook away the cobwebs. His nightmare now made sense. His arms were contorted over his head, still shackled to the rock wall of the cell somewhere in Darcon's fortress, along with John and Ellie.

After being captured by Darcon's forces John and Deacon were hoisted in a giant rope net and flown to the fortress. They made one stop to add another passenger, who was thrown into the net with them. The body flopped like a rag-doll among them. It was Ellie who Deacon feared was dead at first. She had a nice bump on her head and came too later in their uncomfortable flight.

As they winged near to Darcon's fortress, Deacon's heart fell as his fears were realized. Campfires dotted the plane surrounding the stone fortress. The shouting of men and the cry of beasts reached his ears. They were amassing an army prepared for an assault. How were they to fight such unrelenting, oppressive darkness?

The prison door opened with a rusted groan. Shadow warriors stepped through and began unshackling each prisoner.

Ellie rubbed her wrists, glad to be free of the iron manacles. Deacon stretched his shoulders and shot a quick glance at John. He quickly summed up the situation and nodded. Worth a try.

Deacon rushed the first guard and slammed him into the wall, then received a brutal punch to the kidneys from the other guard. John started to move, but the rest of the squad thrust their spears forward, making all thought of further resistance futile.

Chapter 88

Deacon, Ellie, and John shared a nervous glance as the squad of shadow warriors marched them through the labyrinthine halls. Deacon rubbed his back, where he had received the blow to his kidneys.

They reached heavy wood-and-iron doors. The shadow guards on either side of these doors snapped to attention, then pulled the big doors open.

Nasty spears prodded the three prisoners into a vast chamber. At the center of the hall, at the head of a large ornate table, sat Darcon. Torchlight played across his cloak; that same light caused shadows to stretch and waver at the edge of the darkness.

"Ah," Darcon said, standing. "The rest of my guests have arrived. Welcome."

The trio stopped stiffly at the edge of the chamber but was then pushed forward.

It was then Deacon noticed- Darcon was not alone.

Daniel Colson stood uncomfortably. He was utterly out of place. He was tall and thin, with a slight stoop to the shoulders, and quite-unusual clothing. Next to Daniel stood Albright. Deacon wondered how this fragile old man with matted hair and dressed in rags could be involved.

The trio was escorted to the table, which contained a glutton's pile of cooked meats, whole birds, fruits, and vegetables, all piled high.

The shadow warriors moved back into assigned niches in the surrounding walls and stood at attention like dark statues.

Darcon turned to his guests, and with a flourish, said, "Please, be seated!"

Daniel and Albright moved stiffly to the foot of the table and sat. The others did not accept the "hospitality" so quickly.

"We will starve before we sit with you!" Ellie spat.

"Now is that any way to talk to your host?" Darcon replied with a syrupy smile. Then he said with a snarl: "Please leave your dying to me. Now sit down."

Six shadow warriors came forward and forced the three into the remaining chairs.

Darcon turned to Daniel and Albright.

"Professors, these are the leaders of the rebellion. They have caused dissension in my kingdom for years; they don't appreciate my generosity the way you do." As the three riders considered him, Daniel squirmed uncomfortably in his chair. Albright just glared at Darcon, his eyes fiery with rage.

"In fact," Darcon continued, "they would overthrow my kingdom if they could."

"Excuse me," interrupted Ellie. "Whose kingdom?"

"Silence, woman!" Darcon snapped. He wasn't accustomed to such impertinence.

Deacon stood; his chair scraped harshly on the stone floor. "State your business, Darcon!" All six shadow warriors came to alert and moved forward.

John added wryly, "For we are eager to return to those generous accommodations you've afforded us."

Daniel stood slowly, ignoring Albright's attempt to stop him, he interrupted: "Excuse me, but it seems we are the ones who ought to retire. It's obvious you all have matters to discuss —important matters with which we are not involved."

"Oh, you're involved," John said under his breath.

Darcon grinned slyly at Daniel. "More than you know... but we will get to that. Now everyone, sit down! You people are giving me indigestion."

With shadow warriors now having spears at the necks of Ellie and John, Deacon reluctantly sat.

"That's better," Darcon said to Deacon. "As you are aware, I now know where your first stronghold is, and it is only a matter of time before I discover the rest and annihilate your resistance. You are their leader and, if you surrender to me now, you will save your people's lives, as well as your own."

Deacon's smoldering gaze seemed aimed at burning a hole right through this host.

Meanwhile, John responded: "You do not seriously believe we're naïve enough to trust you, do you? And all our people know the price of freedom, as do we. You have played your cards, and the others will not be caught unaware."

"That is spoken confidently for one who will soon be a slave. But your leader sits silent." He turned to Deacon. "Well?"

"No. There is no way in the underworld that I will reveal the strongholds." Deacon stated with finality.

Darcon sighed and smiled tightly. "If you insist. Then you are to be executed in the morning. And after that, we will proceed to obliterate the rest of your little resistance."

He breathed deep, then turned to Daniel and leveled his gaze at him: "Well, now that that's settled... Professor?"

Daniel turned his gaze upon the Dark lord.

"Were you expecting someone to join you?" Darcon asked.

"What?" Daniel asked, unsure of where this was going.

"A few days ago, my men were at the portal, attempting to welcome another traveler. But they were ambushed by our friends here, who kidnapped the arriving Otherlander."

Daniel turned to Deacon. "Is that true?"

"You believe him?" Deacon answered.

Darcon turned to Deacon with a devilish smile. "How is the boy?"

"You bastard!" Ellie shouted, unable to contain herself.

At Darcon's nod, the nearest shadow warrior fiercely backhanded Ellie, knocking her out of her chair. Deacon and John both rocketed to their feet, but the remaining shadow warriors quickly spear-prodded them back down into their seats.

Meanwhile, Daniel stooped to help Ellie up from the floor. As he helped her back into her chair, she whispered to him: "Thomas is safe."

Daniel was dumbfounded by this revelation. *Thomas? Thomas is here? How could he be here? How could he have followed me? What have I done?!*

These thoughts were interrupted by Darcon as he shouted, "Get these savages out of my sight!"

Obedient, six of the room's eight shadow warriors dragged John, Ellie, and Deacon backward toward the open doors. But before reaching them, Deacon vehemently shook off the guards and lasered his defiant glare to meet Darcon's.

Darcon started to scoff, but something from deeper

within him rose and stopped that. Despite his best efforts, his face involuntarily registered something other than confidence, and Deacon saw it.

The shadow guards regained control of Deacon and forced the three prisoners out of the chamber.

Yet while they were still within earshot, Daniel turned to Darcon and demanded, "Where's my son?"

Darcon ignored Daniel. "Can you believe it? They are dead, and I offer them life, but they foolishly throw it back in my face."

"No! You knew my son was here?!"

"Oh, that. Don't worry, my dear professor; I have everything under control."

"That's exactly what worries me." And Daniel stormed toward the other three. One of the remaining shadow guards stepped to block his path, but Daniel slammed into him. Nothing was going to stop him from finding his son.

Darcon looked on, amused. "Let him go. He can do no harm. But follow him and throw him back in the cell." He turned and leveled his gaze on Albright. "Throw them both in their cells. It looks like our professors will be with us for a while."

Chapter 89

Daniel raced into the hall, followed closely by the guards. He saw the trio ahead, being escorted back to the prison area by the shadow warriors.

"Hey! Hold it right there! I want to talk to you."

At Daniel's shout, the three prisoners tried to stop and turn, but the shadow warriors prodded them on with their spears. Daniel caught up and marched alongside them.

"Where is my son?"

"Ellie told you he's safe," Deacon replied flatly.

Daniel glanced at Ellie, who looked to the floor.

"That's not good enough."

"It has to be, for now. We will not jeopardize the security of the resistance."

Grabbing Deacon by the arm, Daniel forcefully spun him around. "Listen! My twelve-year-old son is out there, alone, in a strange land."

Deacon leveled his cold gaze on the distraught father. "You should've thought of that before you left him."

That froze Daniel in his tracks. This stranger was right. He could do nothing but stand and watch as the prisoners were marched on. The weight of the truth bore down on him like a stone monolith from Mairead Fhada.

The shadow guards from the dining chamber caught up with him. One roughly grabbed Daniel by the shoulder and turned him around—right in front of the approaching General Nawg, who leaned down and looked Daniel fiercely in the eye.

"Professor," he hissed, "that is the last time you disrespect my master's hospitality."

Chapter 90

Thomas trudged through the forest. The trees reached together to the sky, forming an almost solid canopy through which only the smallest bit of moonlight shone. *I guess I should be grateful*, thought Thomas. *Even though I can't see, neither can anyone who might be looking for me.*

He stopped and listened. Somewhere there was a rustle in the woods. It was probably a squirrel, or maybe a snake in the leaves. He shuddered at the thought.

He pushed the fear from his mind, willed it to go away, and thought only of his father waiting for him.

The forest thinned. Thomas now could see firelight flickering through the dappled leaves of the trees ahead. He slowed and crept forward from tree to tree. The sounds of shouted orders, clanging weapons, and horses and beasts reached his ears. He finally peeked out of the underbrush into the clearing. It was filled with campfires and tents. Dark men armed for battle and shadow warriors were amassing for war. And beyond the encampment loomed Darcon's stone fortress, massive and dark against the night sky. Thomas quickly pulled back into the protective canopy of the trees.

Chapter 91

"This time I've got it," Deacon said as he inserted a wire into the lock of the prison door. Ellie watched with mild curiosity.

"And… ta-da!" Deacon exclaimed. Then there was a snap. Tight-lipped, Deacon pulled the broken wire out of the lock.

He gave the handle a try. Nothing! Looking at the lock with growing anger, Deacon stood up, grabbed a wooden stool, and smashed it against the metal bars shattering it to pieces. Spent, Deacon crumpled on the floor next to Ellie in frustration.

"Ta-da?" Ellie smirked. Deacon glared at her, then his eyes suddenly filled with a fresh appreciation of her beauty. He could not let her die. He would figure something out. He would rescue them.

Ellie smiled sadly and then turned and stared out the narrow-barred window high on the wall opposite them. Beyond it, the stars were blinking beckoning them to freedom.

Chapter 92

Thomas lay on his stomach in tall grass. He had to rest for a moment. He didn't know how long it had taken him to get this close to the fortress; he only knew he had crawled with tense, painstaking slowness, between the campfires and tents of the amassing army, in fear of the soldiers that moved here and there settling in for the night. Once he was almost stepped on by a horse being led by his master. And now, as he hid prone in the weeds closer to the fortress, he feared one of the sentries along the top of the wall would catch a glimpse of him. So now what?

He could see the castle's entrance, about a hundred yards ahead and to his left. A muddy road led from the forest to the door, which was blocked by a giant iron gate that retracted up into the wall. He remembered his dad had called this a "portcullis."

Thomas saw no way to scale the wall or to squeeze through the portcullis. And could he even cover the distance to the walls without being shot from the wall? He doubted it. The wall, the portcullis, the guards—it all seemed so insurmountable. He was just a boy.

"Oh God, help me," Thomas whispered a desperate prayer, even as he laid his head on the grass in exhaustion.

Something woke him. He must have drifted off. How long had he slept? There was no way of knowing. The moon was high in the sky, hidden by wispy dark clouds. He heard something: the crack of a whip, the creaking of heavy wooden wheels on a bumpy road.

That must have been what awakened him. A fully-loaded wagon was laboriously making its way toward the fortress's entrance. It still had about a hundred yards to go, but it would pass within a few feet of Thomas's grassy hideout.

Meanwhile, at the fortress, the giant chain that suspended the portcullis went taut, and with a rusty groan, the portcullis started rising into the stone wall above it.

Thomas, realizing this opportunity, now crawled rapidly toward the road. The wagon was almost to him. He looked at the open gate, then back at the cart. *This might be my only chance!*

Mustering what little courage he had, he quickly rose into a crouch and scrambled behind the wagon as it passed. Not bothering to check if any guards had seen him, he gently eased onto the wagon's open back, then slipped beneath the covering tarp.

Chapter 93

Deacon, Ellie, and John sat on the cold stone floor of their cell. All were deep in thought.

"All right, all right—we could..." Then Deacon's voice trailed off. He was out of ideas.

"The sun will be up soon," Ellie remarked, peering out the high slit that passed for a window.

"I've got it!" John exclaimed.

"What?" she asked.

"You act sick... ask for some water... you have a fever."

Ellie's face tightened. "Me, pretend? I don't know..."

Deacon turned to her "C'mon, dear Ellie. What have we got to lose?" She blinked at his "dear" greeting.

He was right. They had nothing to lose but their heads.

Chapter 94

Thomas peeked around a corner only to see more dark hallways dimly lit by flickering torches. He didn't really believe he could ever make it into the fortress in the first place. Now he was inside and feared he was hopelessly lost.

Soon he would either be captured by the roving guards or die of starvation.

He had poked his head into numerous doorways and had yet to see any sign of his father, Deacon, Ellie, or John, for that matter.

Thomas started to move again but hesitated as he heard another group of guards coming his way. He ducked behind a wooden keg, and they passed him without notice. Then, as quiet as a mouse, he scurried in the opposite direction.

Chapter 95

A prison guard stood at the prison's outer wooden door as strange female moaning emanated from inside the cell. The guard was unfazed.

The moaning grew louder, but the warrior stayed stolidly at his post. The moan crescendoed, transforming to a shriek.

Inside the cell, John cradled Ellie in his arms. "Hey! Out there! You've got a sick prisoner in here!"

Ellie wailed like a banshee.

"She has a fever!" John gasped. "Or worse... we need some water!"

The outer door opened; the guard peered through the bars.

"Come on!" Deacon demanded. "If she dies, it's your problem. You'll have robbed your master of the pleasure of killing her. I'd bring that water if I were you."

The guard disappeared.

Deacon, Ellie, and John exchanged a glance. Maybe this was working.

The guard reappeared, carrying a bucket of water. He stepped through the cell's outer door.

Deacon stood clenching his fist, ready to spring at the guard the moment the cell door opened. "You did the right thing. Now if you will just—"

Splash! The guard threw the entire contents of the bucket in Deacon's face, but it drenched John and Ellie as well.

So they just stared, dripping and dumbfounded. And the guard gave a hint of a smile before he exited, with a loud slam of the enormous outer door.

Outside, in the fortress's courtyard, the rising sun glinted off the big blade of an ax, being pressed to knife sharpness against a grindstone.

Deacon, John, and Ellie sat silently in their cell. The outer door opened to reveal General Nawg. "It's time."

———

Deacon, John, and Ellie marched down the hall toward their demise. Ellie glanced nervously at Deacon. "I'm still thinking," he responded.

Chapter 96

In the great hall, Darcon leaned forward on his dais. His voice echoed across the chamber, "Dr. Colson, give me the way back through the portal!"

Daniel responded flatly. "No."

Daniel knew the only way to stay alive was to keep Darcon thinking he had discovered the way back, even though he hadn't actually cracked the combination. He didn't know if his charade could last much longer.

"What?"

"Since coming here, I've learned how much you've stained this land with blood. No, Darcon, I am leaving you here to get what you deserve."

Darcon flinched slightly, just for a second, then whispered: "Ah. The clever Professor Colson."

Daniel watched as Darcon pushed his hood back and revealed the face and white hair of a hard-lived man in his late sixties. His face profoundly wrinkled and almost beached in its whiteness. "I knew it was only a matter of time until you figured me out... I see no need to keep you in the dark regarding my identity any longer."

Daniel stared, and then the puzzle fell into place. What he had suspected was now confirmed. "Michael Avery of Scotland. Professor of Medieval studies, Edinburgh." Daniel smiled, grimly. "We all thought you were dead."

"It has been more than 30 years since I came through the portal."

Daniel's mind reeled again at the time properties of the portal.

"Yes, professor. The portal seems to have a mind of its own."

Darcon turned to the fire. "And how did you finally solve the enigma that is the stone circle, Mairead Fhada?" Darcon used the ancient Gaelic tongue. "Or what the locals of Umbria called it, Long Meg and Her Daughters."

"I read your book," Daniel replied.

Darcon laughed. "They all said I was a fool, I was losing my mind. Thinking the stone circles were portals. Like I was some Alice in Wonderland going down the rabbit hole."

"I went to your funeral. It was my first week of university."

Darcon softened at this for a moment.

"How did I die?"

"It was assumed you took your life," Daniel answered. "Threw yourself in the river."

"Ah, of course. I can hear them now. Professor Avery, your much learning has driven you mad," Darcon smirked.

"Your book was why I came to Cambridge, it set me on my academic path. Without it, I would not have pursued the constellation patterns as timing to open the door."

Darcon smiled. "Yes, good work that." A hint of his Scottish accent came through.

"It was brilliant," Daniel responded.

"Do you remember our great poet Wordsworth? Of

Course you do. He wrote a verse about our stone circle, Long Meg."

Daniel nodded, unsure of this more humane Darcon.

Darcon turned back to the fire and gazing into it began:

> *"A weight of Awe not easy to be borne*
> *Fell suddenly upon my spirit, cast*
> *From the dread bosom of the unknown past,*
> *When first I saw that family forlorn;*
> *Speak Thou, whose massy strength and stature*
> *   scorn*
> *The power of years - pre-eminent, and placed*
> *Apart, to overlook the circle vast.*
> *Speak Giant-mother! Tell it to the Morn,*
> *While she dispels the cumbrous shades of night;*
> *Let the Moon hear, emerging from a cloud,*
> *At whose behest uprose on British ground*
> *That Sisterhood in hieroglyphic round*
> *Forth-shadowing, some have deemed the infinite*
> *The inviolable God that tames the proud."*

Darcon pulled something from the folds of his robe and gazed at it longingly.

"We loved to walk among her stones in the early fog. The sun would rise over the hills of Umbria, and in that in-between time, we would talk of our dreams, our future."

Darcon slipped the item back into his robe, and Daniel had a glimpse. It was a photograph, yellowed with age and tattered at the edges.

"It was there on those misty mornings that the legend of Mairead Fhada, Long Meg and Her Daughters, got a hold of me, and she would not let go."

Daniel knew the legend all too well. How it was said

that Long Meg and her daughters were a coven of witches who were holding their sabbath, when the Scottish wizard Michael Scot, came upon them and turned them to stone. The stones of the circle are said to be uncountable, and that should anyone ever reach the same total twice, that the spell would be broken and the stones would turn back to women.

Local history also told the tale of the local squire who tried to remove the stones. As the work started, a tremendous and terrifying storm broke out overhead, which caused the work to be permanently abandoned.

"The legend of Michael of Scotland," Daniel said.

"Yes, yes. Michael of Scotland. Did you know he was my ancestor?" Darcon smiled. "I was named after him. It was said he disappeared after his battle with Long Meg and her coven of witch daughters." Darcon took on the air of a lecturing professor.

"I wondered if there were any elements of the story that could be true. Not, of course, the rubbish about witches and people being turned to stone. No, those were stories created later to frighten people away from the door. Could the legends of the thinning of the mist between worlds be real? And what of the strange storms that seemed to come at various times throughout the decades?"

Daniel couldn't help but be awed by the origin of this man's journey. "And so you began your search."

"Yes. And I wrote my book." Darcon turned to Daniel with a snarl. "That's when the laughter began. At first, it was little comments I would hear spoken in whispers in the dining hall of the college. Then, the chuckles at faculty gatherings. The invitations stopped coming to those gatherings. I was passed over for department positions. Finally, I realized that only my tenure kept me from being released."

Darcon put his hand absentmindedly into the upper fold of his robe near his heart.

"Only one person believed in me." He withdrew his hand, clutching the tattered photograph and gazed at it longingly. "Helen." He whispered.

"Your wife."

"Her love, her admiration should have been enough." Darcon's voice dropped. "It wasn't." Darcon slumped back into his high wooden chair upon the dais.

"I left her one night in October. I came through the portal."

Darcon straightened and turned back to Daniel. "Professor Colson, I must insist. I need the way through that door, and I'm counting on you to supply it."

"Professor Avery, please. Stop this madness!"Daniel pleaded.

The man in the ornate wooden chair stood barely containing his rage. "My name is Darcon!" He hissed, "You will open the door for me!"

"I owe you nothing."

"Professor, you think you know me? I may have been a mere intellect on earth, but here I am, Lord!"

"Then, why go back?"

"Oh, I'm not going back to stay," Darcon smiled.

Daniel asked, "Just to get some modern trinkets of power, for more effective oppression of the people here?"

"Well said, Professor Colson. With such thinking, we could work well together."

"And how is it you knew the way to get here, but you have yet to figure out the way back?"

"A minor detail," Darcon admitted, "that I overlooked in my zeal to transfer here. You see, I assumed the original deciphering of the 'combination' to the portal would work the same in both directions. Clever, those who designed it, and I'm counting on you to be just as clever."

Darcon turned to the fire again. "Yes, I was overzealous then. But surely, now that you and your son are trapped here, you can understand my zeal to return."

"Such zeal has now caused two planets great pain. And your impatient rushing ahead triggered mine. First, you asked, 'could we?' not 'should we?' and then I idiotically followed suit. Without such impatience, perhaps both of us could have been great scientists."

"Unless we get out of here, neither of us will be so known, and I've learned enough ruthlessness here that I suspect I can surpass you wherever we are."

This made Daniel feel pity, but Darcon took it as empathy. He softened and, looking almost poignant, said: "Professor, is there no way I can persuade you to help me?"

But the flames cast a strange shadow over Darcon's face, and Daniel quickly responded: "No, no way. From what I've seen here, nothing could ever make me give you the pattern."

Darcon narrowed his eyes and said smugly: "So you say. But like I said, I've learned ruthlessness." And he gestured to the door.

The guards there opened them, and two more shadow warriors roughly dragged Thomas in. Thomas fearfully glanced around, then saw Daniel. "Dad!" Thomas shouted.

And Daniel started to move to his son but discovered two shadow warriors had come up and restrained him.

"Thomas!"

Thomas struggled in the guards' grips.

"Dad, I followed you."

Daniel turned to Darcon. "Let him go."

Darcon nodded. The warriors released their grip. Thomas rushed to his father, and Daniel scooped up his boy in a mighty hug.

"Thomas, are you all right?"

"Yes... Dad, why did you leave us?"

"I was a selfish fool. Son, will you forgive me? I will never leave you again."

Daniel stepped back from his son, holding him by the shoulders. As he did, he noticed something swing out between the lapels of Thomas's jacket. It was the pendant Loren had given Thomas.

Daniel immediately recognized the Trinitarian Celtic circle intertwined with the Dragon. He started to say something, but quickly remembered their predicament and closed his mouth.

Thomas looked at his father. "I love you, Dad. And I forgive you."

"Son, I don't deserve you."

Darcon's patience was exhausted. "How sweet... but enough!"

The shadow warriors tore Daniel and Thomas apart.

"No. Dad!"

"Hey, take it easy!" Daniel demanded of the guards as they dragged his son back.

"Thomas, we're going to be okay. You'll see. We are going to get through this."

Darcon stepped between the father and his son, then turned and spoke to Thomas like a kindly uncle. "Thomas, your father, and I have some business to finish, and then you may go home. Isn't that right, professor?"

Daniel considered his son. What else could he do?

"Yes," Daniel answered, never taking his eyes from Thomas.

An older bearded male servant entered along with Mia.

Mia snuck a glance at Daniel, and their eyes connected for a moment, then she quickly averted her attention.

"Master, they are ready to begin."

"Good!" Darcon exclaimed. "I'm so glad both of you could be here for this... curtains, please."

The slave girl, Mia, and the older bearded slave drew back heavy drapes, and harsh sunlight filled the room. Beyond the thick curtains stood large ornate doors. They were opened onto a large balcony, which looked down three stories onto the fortress's courtyard.

Darcon stepped to the balcony and motioned for Daniel and Thomas to join him. The guards thrust the Earthlings forward.

As Thomas stepped out, he could see the entire court-yard. At its center stood a raised wooden platform. Around the base of the platform were hundreds of human soldiers in dark armor emblazoned with the crimson writhing serpent of Darcon and shadow warriors standing in formation.

Daniel and Thomas were forced into their chairs on the balcony. Darcon smiled at father and son, then said with a flourish: "Let the executions begin."

Chapter 97

Gears turned, and chains groaned; at the side end of the courtyard, one of the iron portcullis raised into the stone wall. General Nawg emerged from the darkness, followed by Deacon, Ellie, and John, along with their guard squad of shadow warriors.

"Deacon!" Thomas shouted, jumping to his feet.

The three friends looked up at the boy. Ellie gave him a sad smile. Then their attention was turned back to the solemn task at hand.

Rough hands pushed Thomas back into his seat. Daniel pulled his agonized son close, attempting to comfort him and shared a solemn glance with Albright.

Deacon, John, and Ellie were marched onto the platform. The burly executioner waited there, leaning on a huge ax, his face covered in a black hood. Deacon was shoved forward. Shadow warriors snapped metal cuffs onto his wrist and locked a chain around his neck.

Watching the resistance's mighty leader forced to his knees, Darcon gloated as the guards threaded the chain from Deacon's neck through the wrist cuffs to a ring in front of an ancient wooden block stained black from years of executions.

"More wine! My goblet is empty." Darcon ordered, and the slave girl Mia immediately brought a pitcher to comply.

As Deacon kneeled, he offered a comforting smile up at Ellie and John. A tear rolled down Ellie's cheek.

Deacon laid his neck on the block.

The executioner took his place. He adjusted his grip on the ax's leather-wrapped handle, then looked to his master on the balcony.

Darcon smiled—enjoying his victory, savoring the fall of his long-time foe, who had nipped at Darcon's heels since Deacon was only fourteen yours old. This thorn would finally be extracted from his side. He stood and raised his goblet. His voice echoed in the courtyard, "To the leader of the resistance. How the mighty have fallen!"

The bloodthirsty warriors assembled there shouted and clashed their shields and swords. Darcon raised his hand for silence. Then he nodded, and the executioner lifted the ax high; it glinted in the morning sun.

Thomas could not bear to watch and bowed his head.

Ellie turned her face away.

Deacon closed his eyes.

The executioner drew back to swing the ax down with force. At that moment, a dragon's trumpet echoed through the fortress.

Deacon's eyes flashed open. "Thorn!"

The deadly ax fell, but Deacon jerked back—making the chain that bound him taut across the chopping block. Sparks flew as the executioner's ax severed the chain.

Deacon was free!

Deacon jumped to his feet and slugged the blinking executioner, who fell like a stone. Deacon looked to the sky in amazement to see Thorn leading an army of dragons and their riders, all armed for battle.

Thorn trumpeted his battle cry. And hundreds of dragons answered his call like a mighty roll of thunder.

Chapter 98

"For the kingdom!" Tuncan shouted, and the riders of the resistance echoed in unison, as they poured over the walls.

A shadow-warrior sentry put a horn to his lips to sound the alarm, but thwip!—he was shot in the throat by an arrow. Other guards along the fortress wall were plucked from the wall by giant talons.

"For the kingdom!" Mia, the slave girl, shouted to the other slaves, and servants then swung her wine pitcher, crashing it into the head of the nearest guard. Seeing her bravery and emboldened by her cry, the slaves and servants took up the call and joined into the resistance.

Realizing the enormity of the rebel forces, General Nawg turned from the battle and slipped down some dark stairs that burrowed into the fortress wall.

Coming awake, the executioner watched the sky as the dragons and their riders came. Then he turned to where his prisoner should have been, only to see Deacon now holding the ax, shifting it from hand to hand.

The executioner started to rise, but he barely got to his

T. KEVIN BRYAN

knees before Deacon swung the flat of the ax right at his face; the executioner's nose broke, and he toppled unconscious off the dais.

Ellie spun with her hands, clasped together, and gave a powerful uppercut to the shadow warrior coming up from behind her. As he fell, she grabbed the hilt of his sword and pulled it from its sheath.

John's dragon, the mighty red Krag, approached. "Come on, Krag!"

John leaped into the saddle, and he and Krag took to the sky to join the resistance.

Deacon watched them go, then turned to Ellie with a smirk: "I told you I would think of something."

Ellie grabbed Deacon and, pulling him to her, gave him a big kiss. "I knew you would!" she yelled as she jumped off the dais and into the battle.

Deacon was speechless. Then he re-hefted the executioner's ax and followed his partner's leaped into the battle.

On the balcony above the courtyard, Darcon watched in dismay as his plans began to crumble. "Seize them!" he ordered, pointing at Daniel and Thomas. The guard next to Daniel turned, but Daniel was too swift.

He stood and, grabbing his chair, smashed it against the shadow warrior's head. The warrior rocked back on his heels for a moment, then Albright gave him a shove with all his might, the being tumbled over the balcony's edge; it landed far below with a bone-crunching thud.

Daniel turned to grab Thomas, but then his heart felt like it had stopped. He was staring at Darcon, who held Thomas tightly and had his wicked blade pressed to the boy's throat.

Thomas squirmed. "Dad!"

Daniel moved toward his son.

"Don't!" Darcon tightened his grip. "Perhaps this would be a good time to finish our business." Darcon turned to the remaining guards and said: "Help the others. The professor will give me no more trouble. Will you, professor?"

Chapter 99

The battle raged on. John, atop his dragon, hacked a shadow warrior in the ribs. Then an arrow sliced through the air piercing John's thigh. John grabbed the arrow and, grimacing, broke off the shaft.

He looked up as another arrow whizzed past him. He followed the line of its trajectory and saw a shadow warrior bearing down on him, another arrow at the ready.

John urged on his dragon and pulled out a spear lashed to the side of his saddlebag. He readied it as a jouster would. He felt another arrow streak past him as he soared toward the shadow warrior.

"Steady, boy!" John encouraged his dragon.

The dragons collided mid-air. John's spear impaled the shadow warrior, who was thrust from his dragon and fell spinning to the ground.

In the courtyard, amidst the battle, Deacon and Ellie stood back-to-back fighting shadow warriors.

Ellie looked to the balcony. She saw Darcon pulling Thomas into the fortress, with Daniel following and the old man, Albright, as well.

"Deacon!" Ellie nodded to the balcony. "Thomas."

Deacon looked in time to see them disappear into the darkness.

"Where is he taking him?" Ellie asked.

"I assume 'twill be the Door. I'll get him," he assured her as he stabbed another opponent, then looked to the sky and whistled.

Thorn had been busy dispatching shadow-warrior archers and other guards; hearing his master's call, he spun in the sky and dove. Coming in fast, the big dragon dropped hard on the warrior Ellie was fighting, crushing him into the ground.

"Not bad," Deacon said, admiring Thorn's landing. Deacon then leaped into the saddle.

Giving Ellie a smile, he grabbed the reins and commanded: "Up, Thorn." And his giant friend again, eagerly, took to the sky.

———

Darcon pulled Thomas along a dark passage. The boy's feet barely touched the cobbled floor. Daniel followed, hoping against hope he could somehow save his son.

———

Outside, the fortress was engulfed in flames. The battle continued to rage on the ground and in the air. Swords clashed their iron blades reflecting the burning fortress's light.

Chapter 100

Ellie heroically fought another shadow warrior even though spent. The warrior swung his mighty sword with both hands. Ellie blocked the blow, but the force drove her to the ground. She was done, and the warrior's next blow would kill her.

He raised his wicked blade for her finish... then shuddered and fell forward atop her, with an arrow's shaft protruding out of his back.

Ellie struggled to push the body off, then saw Tuncan and his dragon diving to her rescue... just as burning timbers from the execution platform fell toward her.

Tuncan bent in his saddle and, grabbing her, swung Ellie into the seat behind him. They soared into the sky as the burning platform collapsed to the ground.

———

Darcon continued dragging Thomas along. They descended steps chiseled out of the rock, and the passage turned to a cave.

Deacon and Thorn flew over the forest. Smoke from the fully-engulfed fortress hung in the distance behind them. As they neared a forest-covered hillock, a massive black dragon rose from it and blocked their path. Astride it was General Nawg.

Deacon reined up Thorn, and the two dragons hovered as they and their riders considered each other. Then, with a kick from each the dragons charged.

Darcon, Thomas, and Daniel continued through the cave. Thomas noticed it seemed to be getting brighter. They turned a corner, and ahead of them was an opening.

"Almost there," Darcon said.

"Where are you taking us?" Daniel asked.

"You'll see soon enough, professor."

The cave's mouth opened, and they stepped into the light and a clearing at the edge of a dense forest. There stood the monolithic stones of this world's "Mairead Fhada," waiting patiently like silent sentries.

Daniel followed close behind, remembering how he had come through the portal only a month earlier. Darcon dragged Thomas the rest of the distance to the stones. Moving himself and the boy to the center of the stone circle, Darcon stood marveling at them.

Chapter 101

As Deacon and Nawg crossed swords, iron flashed in the mid-air sunlight.

"You may as well surrender," Deacon shouted from atop Thorn. "You know it is over!" And he deftly parried a strike by the shadow warriors' dark leader.

"Never!" hissed Nawg.

Their dragons turned and swooped toward each other for another attack. This time, just before they collided, Deacon stood in his saddle and launched himself onto the back of Nawg's black beast.

Deacon swung his sword, but Nawg blocked it, then stabbed so close to Deacon's right eye that Deacon's avoidance caused him to slide off the beast's back. In the nick of time, he caught hold of the dark dragon's saddle straps.

Hanging precariously, Deacon desperately looked for an advantage, while Nawg stabbed his sword downward on either side, hoping to wound Deacon. But while Nawg was searching for the correct angle, Deacon saw his opportunity and plunged his blade deep into Nawg's dragon's heart.

As its black blood spurted, the beast let out a death-crying scream, then spun and fell, out of control. Nawg attempted to hold on. Deacon just grinned at his adversary, even as he released his grip on the beast's harness and dropped into space.

Watching Nawg and his beast spinning, Deacon fell several hundred feet before he remembered his precarious state and yelled: "Thorn?!"

Thorn trumpeted as he dove from the sky and snagged his falling master in his claws.

The black beast crashed into the ground with a cloud of dust and earth.

Deacon, now in the saddle, reined Thorn in. They landed near the ruined beast. General Nawg was nowhere to be seen. Deacon dismounted and cautiously walked the perimeter of the black dragon's carcass.

He looked down and saw Nawg's black cloak protruding from under the dragon's black-bleeding side. He stooped to fold back the cloth; he had to be sure Nawg was dead.

Behind Deacon, Nawg silently reverted into his physical form and lifted his sword to strike. But Deacon saw his nemesis' shadow and spun in time to dodge Nawg's sword while thrusting his own.

Nawg fell against Deacon, face to neck. Deacon bore the shadow warrior's weight, then pushed him back. That's when he saw his thrust had impaled Nawg, who was no more. After pushing Nawg's body to the ground, Deacon wiped his blade on the grass, then slid it back into its sheath.

Deacon climbed into the saddle, patted Thorn on the neck, and said: "We must off to get Thomas."

Thorn bugled his affirmation, then the giant dragon

leaped into the air, and they flew on to help their young friend.

Chapter 102

"It's incredible, isn't it?" Darcon marveled at the standing stones.

He stood in the center of their circle, one hand gripping Thomas's shoulders and the other holding his knife near Thomas's throat. "That something so rustic, so ancient, could contain such power? And now its secret will be mine."

He turned to Daniel. "Professor?"

"As soon as you release my son," Daniel responded, never ceasing to stare into Thomas's eyes.

"In due time, professor."

Thomas kept looking for some advantage. It seemed hopeless. Was it true that your life flashed before your eyes in dangerous moments? He did know that people and relationships did. He thought of all his anger. He had been angry at that kid in Britain. At Deacon. At his dad for leaving. Maybe even God. Thomas decided at that moment. He would grow up. And then Thomas had a sudden revelation. He was angry with all the wrong people. He should be mad at this Darcon guy. And that is who he should fight like Deacon and the resistance.

He would resist the evil in his own heart, and he would fight this evil man that stood now restraining him. But what could he do? Then he saw it. Darcon's forearm was wrapped in front of Thomas's neck.

Thomas sunk his teeth into Darcon's left forearm.

Darcon screamed, "Argh!"

Daniel rushed forward.

"Stay back!" Darcon demanded. He ignored his teeth-marked forearm, moved it across Thomas's chest, then pressed his knife, so it pricked Thomas's throat. The boy grimaced but focused on his father and stood bravely.

Despite the sharp blade pressing against his soft neck Thomas said, "Dad, I'm okay."

Daniel stopped but now glared fierily into the eyes of the man who held his son. "If you hurt him, I swear I'll kill you."

———

"We have the victory!" Ellie shouted to Deacon from atop the small Splinter.

"Not yet!" Deacon nodded to the ground beneath them, where Daniel, Albright, Thomas, and Darcon stood among the standing stones.

"Down, Thorn!"

The dragons and riders descended, but not so swiftly as to make Darcon flinch.

Chapter 103

"Open the door, Professor, Now!" Darcon barked.

Dad?" Thomas cringed as the knife pressed against his neck.

"Open the door!" Darcon repeated.

"Okay, okay... Thomas, you're going to be all right," Daniel reassured.

Just then, beyond the stony circle, Thorn landed. Deacon sprung from the saddle and sprinted toward his friends.

Seeing his old nemesis approaching, Darcon threatened: "Stay back, or the boy is dead!"

Ellie was also running toward Thomas, but Deacon stopped her and commanded: "Darcon, it's over. Let the boy go."

"You stay out of this. This is between the professor and myself."

Deacon and Ellie looked nervously at Daniel and Thomas.

With a heavy sigh, Daniel began to direct Darcon.

"Start at that stone." Daniel pointed to the twelve-foot

high "Long Meg," the tallest of the moss-covered monoliths.

Darcon dragged Thomas to the stone his father had indicated.

As he did, dark clouds rolled in from out of nowhere. Both Darcon and Thomas looked up. Darcon smiled; even after thirty years, he remembered the electric thrill of the portal.

Thomas, on the other hand, hated what was happening. He attempted to jerk away from Darcon but was held fast. The pendant slipped from out of Thomas' jacket and arced out on its chain, glinting for a moment like a drop of sunshine then rested back on Thomas' chest.

Albright saw it. "The key," he gasped. Albright turned to Daniel, barely able to contain himself. "Your son has the key."

Daniel nodded solemnly. He had seen it.

Albright closed his eyes and began to whisper to himself almost as if in prayer.

"When the veil is thin, and the warrior is armed..."

Albright's eyes flashed open, and he repeated,

"When the veil is thin, and the warrior is armed." Almost willing the boy to know what to do.

Thomas, still clutched by Darcon, looked down at the gold Trinitarian pendant that now protruded from his jacket. Later he would say it was like an echo from far away he heard the verse. He whispered to himself through barely parted lips.

"When the veil is thin, and the warrior is armed..." Thomas grasped the pendant in his hand and suddenly remembered the dying words of his friend Loren as he had given him the pendant: "And this will help you find the way. There are ancient stories told of an Otherlander. One who would bear the pendant and drive the darkness from our land. He knows the secret of the pendant. It unlocks the door through the mist to Otherland, your world."

Albright standing deathly still continued," …walk the path of the Creator."

Daniel shouted, "Now, in a sun-wise direction, begin walking around the inside of the stone circle."

Thomas stood frozen, still in the grip of Darcon.

"Continue walking in the circle," Daniel directed. "Thomas, it's okay, show him the pattern!"

"No, Dad!" he beseeched. "I won't go without you!"

"Thomas, you must. Your mother is waiting for you, and I will find you, no matter what!"

Darcon prodded the boy. "Get on with it!"

Thomas searched his mind for the rest of the verse. "Walk the path of the creator," he whispered silently.

Thomas cringed and took a hesitant step. With a blinding CRACK! Lightning struck the monolith known on earth as "Long Meg." And Thomas continued walking the Trinitarian pattern: The Pattern discovered by his father. The pattern he had walked, which had brought him to this strange world. But why was it working now? This was not tied to any astronomical event that he could discern. It had to be the pendant. The pendant was the key. The key that would open the door to his world! All these thoughts rushed through Thomas' mind as he continued the leaf-like threefold symmetrical pattern. Darcon followed behind with his hand locked on Thomas's shoulder.

Thomas whispered the ancient verse to himself as he shuffled along.

"Destruction awaits he
Who steps to the right or left."

Lightning flashed. Thunder rolled.

Thomas apprehensively looked from the gathering

storm to his father as he and Darcon continued their deadly game of follow the leader. As they passed each stone, lightning struck it with a crack and a sizzle. But the flash also illumined and held the stone in its surging, humming grip.

Darcon continued pushing his unwilling hostage along toward the next stone in the pattern. "Thomas!" Daniel shouted over the storm, just as another bolt struck that next stone... and held it with a hum.

"Thomas, listen to me!" Another surging-and-holding flash of lightning, and a delayed clap of thunder.

"Son, I won't ever—"

Lightning on the next stone drowned out Daniel's finale to that sentence, and now all the stones were held in the lightning's grip. The humming and surging were deafening. Thomas looked with fear again at his father. He could see him shouting, but the increasing power of the cosmic forces drowned out his voice.

Thomas knew what was coming. Then he saw the old man, his father's friend with eyes closed mouthing words. And it hit him.

"Destruction awaits he

Who steps to the right or left"

Many things seemed to happen at once. All of it was in hyper-slow motion to Thomas.

Thomas looked up at Darcon and saw that he was enraptured by the cosmic electrical forces surrounding them. He felt the tyrant's hand loosen its grip on his shoulder, and Darcon's awe of the power around him caused his knife hand to relax.

Thomas anger welled up in him and he pushed the evil tyrant with all his might, and at that, Daniel leaped forward and knocked Thomas from Darcon's grasp, forcing him to the ground and sheltering his body.

Darcon then lashed out and swung madly at Daniel but instead plunged his knife into the back of Albright, who had rushed at the moment he saw Thomas move.

Daniel shoved Thomas out of the circumference of the stone circle, and Deacon grabbed Albright, pulling him as well as the lightning streaked from all the stones and struck Darcon.

Surging through Darcon's rising body, this time, the bolts of lightning caused their target to writhe in agony, though his scream could not be heard.

Ellie watched in stunned amazement, Daniel rose, pulled Thomas to his feet, dragged him to a sprint, and shouted to the others, "Run!"

They all dashed away from the circle of glowing mono-liths, just as the umbrella of lightning surged to a peak of power and exploded, making Darcon disappear and expelling a concussive blast that knocked them all to the surrounding ground.

The dust cleared.

Deacon stood and checked on Ellie then gently helped her to her feet. "You all right, love?"

"Yes." They hugged tightly.

Daniel and Thomas checked themselves for damage. Daniel looked his son over, brushed the hair back from his face, then enveloped the boy in a fierce hug.

"Everyone all right?" Ellie asked.

Thomas looked from his dad to Ellie. "Yeah, I am now."

It was then that Thomas heard a groan. They all searched, and Deacon yelled," Over here."

Daniel rushed to his friend's side. He cradled his head. "Albright, You stupid fool."

Albright smiled and gazed up at Daniel." Dr. Colson, it was my turn to follow you."

Thomas looked on, feeling his heart might break at any moment.

Daniel muttered, "Albright, you're going to be okay, hang in there, old friend."

Albright smirked, "Old, why I'm twenty years your junior Doctor."

He grimaced as a wave of pain passed over his features.

"Dr. Colson, it is time for me to go now."

"No," Thomas groaned.

"It's okay, take your dad home and say give your mom a hug. It's my turn to go through the door. And I know someone is waiting for me." His voice trailed off, and he breathed his last.

Daniel reached and pulling Thomas into an embrace, wept.

Thomas stood, staring into the charred circle inside the stones. "It doesn't look like Darcon made it."

"No, he didn't," Daniel responded, shaking his head soberly.

"What happened?" asked Ellie.

"He took a wrong turn," Daniel muttered.

Chapter 104

It was a glorious morning. Thomas watched as the sun rose over the tops of the circle of monoliths. The fog of the early morning dissipated, but the air was still crisp and refreshing. He stood with his dad, Deacon, Ellie, and John, quietly at the graveside of Albright, which was covered with a heap of stones. A host of others from the resistance had gathered respectfully, all crowded among the Monoliths. After his father quoted Psalm Twenty-three, Ellie laid wildflowers at the head of the grave. Then she straightened looked at the sunrise sang a haunting ballad in her ancient tongue. Thomas, for the rest of his life, thought it was the most beautiful moment he ever knew. He wanted to cry, to laugh to jump and be still all at once. For him, it was the beginning of understanding the essence of real joy. Deep contentment knowing that even though suffering had come, he was all right. It was the beginning of understanding trust. He could trust his father. He could trust his friends. He could trust his God.

Thomas walked slowly over to Thorn. The dragon

dipped his head to the boy. "Goodbye, Thorn," Thomas said, as he hugged his giant friend's neck.

Thorn rumbled his acknowledgment.

Ellie came, bent over, then kissed Thomas on the cheek.

The boy blushed and said, "Thank you."

"No, Thomas. Thank you."

Deacon extended his hand. "Farewell, Thomas."

Thomas took Deacon's hand. Then, surprising the man, the boy pulled him into a hug.

"I'm going to miss you."

"As am I."

Deacon stood and shook Daniel's hand. "We fought Darcon physically for years. Clearly, what we needed was someone who could outsmart him."

"Well, we can all be thankful he never got his hands on Loren's pendant, or things would've turned out differently."

Thomas looked at the pendant Loren gave him, and couldn't help but be sad. He traced the circular pattern on the pendant, then brightened. "Yeah, Dad says I get to navigate on the way back." He looked at his father with a big smile.

Chapter 105

Caroline placed a bouquet of freshly picked flowers on the grass, then stood and gazed up at Mairead Fhada's ancient monoliths. She had hope. Caroline had too. That was the only way she could go on, waiting for the return of her husband and son.

She turned her back on the stones and walked out of the circle. But when she was only two steps outside it, thunder clapped, and Caroline's back was buffeted by a blast of wind.

She turned back to the stones and froze in disbelief and joy as she saw Daniel and Thomas standing at the center of the stone circle.

Thomas shook his head, clearing it from vertigo… then he saw the most beautiful sight he had ever seen: His mother, running to him. He sprinted to her, and they embraced. They both were enwrapped by Daniel.

Looking up, Caroline gazed at her husband. "I knew you would come back."

Daniel kissed his wife softly, then pulled both wife and

son as close and tight as he could. He knew he would never let them go like this again. Thomas gazed up at his mother and father. "We're home."

"Yes, son," Daniel agreed. "We are home."

Epilogue

Searing pain, white-hot. It slowly receded. Was he dead? Was this hell? No.

Now Darcon could perceive he was resting on jagged rocks. They pushed into his shoulder blades. His skin and bones all ached; this convinced him he was alive.

Water lapped at his side. He sat up and peered into the mist. He was on gray crags, lapped at by an ocean. All was shrouded.

Then he remembered: He had been deceived. Robbed. His chance to return to his homeland was forever lost. His power over N'albion gone. His lips curled.

But then another vision struck him, of what he had glimpsed as he slammed through the door. Before crossing the threshold, in the mist of the time between times, he had seen a faint outline of the future: A figure, in a dragon rider's jacket, with sword drawn. Darcon could feel the cold steel impale him; he rubbed his abdomen in spite of himself.

As the dragon rider withdrew the sword and turned

away, the motion made something swing free of his leather jacket. A pendant. The pendant!

A terrible resolve filled Darcon. He knew what he must do.

He would find a way back.

He would destroy the Pendant-Bearer.

He would kill Thomas, the Otherlander.

Through the Storm

Thomas, Deacon and Thorn will return in—

OTHERLANDER
Book 2
Through the Storm

"Yank, go home!" The pitcher shouted at Thomas as he stood holding his cricket bat in front of the wickets. Thomas glared back at the pitcher and tightened his grip on the bat.

"Bowl him out, Arnie!" Added one of the fielders. They adjusted their positions, waiting for their captain to throw the ball at the wickets.

Thomas couldn't help but remember how he used to feel about this game: Frightened of the ball, unsure of the rules, the last kid to ever be picked to play on a team, he would have rather died than play cricket last year. But this was a whole new year. And he felt like a whole new Thomas.

He was forced to grow up fast. He had only been gone about a week in earth days. But he had lived a lifetime in N'albion. Somewhere beyond the mist. Somewhere on the other side of the storm.

In his search for his missing father, Thomas was catapulted through the portal that was the stone circle known in ancient Scotland as "Mairead Fhada." He found himself in another place, a medieval world filled with noble warriors that rode dragons and their archenemies, the dark shadow warriors.

If Thomas knew then what he knew now: the dangers he would experience, the terrifying battles he would endure, would he have gone? He had to believe that he would. What other choice was there? He was just thankful to God that he found his father and they both made it home safely to his mother. He could hardly consider what it would have been like to face his mother if he had come home empty-handed. He banished the thought from his head. God did answer his prayer and brought them both safely back. And now there was something else that brought great joy to their house, his mother was pregnant. He was going to be a big brother. The baby was due around Christmas. Maybe that was what he was getting for Christmas. He couldn't help but smile at that. England wasn't so bad after all.

"What are you grinning about Thomas?" taunted the pitcher.

"This Yank is about to go home…run!"

Arnie rolled his eyes at the American baseball reference, then wound up, took three quick steps forward, leaped into the air, and hurled the ball. The ball took a bounce a few feet before reaching Thomas. Thomas swung with all his might. The bat connected with a crack and the ball streaked into the sky. The fielders scrambled for position moving further back, back again as they followed the arc of the ball until finally, they could go no farther, and they bounced off the outfield fence. Their hearts sank as the ball dropped in the grass 10 feet on the other side. Thomas' team cheered crazily and rushed Thomas, grabbed him and hoisted him onto their shoulders.

"That counts for six runs!" Harry complained, slamming his cap on the ground and sending up a cloud of dust.

Arnie watched as Thomas was carried off the field by his rejoicing team.

"Funny that."

"What?" asked Harry picking up his hat.

"It's like that Yank is a whole new Yank."

Acknowledgments

It is with great joy that I finish this first novel. It has been a lengthy undertaking and not without its challenges. I did not do it alone. I must thank the many family and friends who listened to me go on and on about the story. Thank you for your patience and encouragement. Tim Mercer designed the cover and did a marvelous job. My son, Hayden, spent many Saturday morning doing writing sessions with me and is a fantastic storyteller in his own right. And of course, my wife, Linda, my incredible companion, friend, and partner. I indeed married up! Thank you all!

T. Kevin Bryan

T. Kevin Bryan is an emerging author of Fantasy. Kevin lives in a little house in California with his wife and son and a Border Terrier named Sherlock.

Be sure and continue reading Thomas the Otherlander's adventures in "Through the Storm"

Find out more at tkevinbryan.com

Also by T. Kevin Bryan

OTHERLANDER Book 2

Through the Storm

Coming in 2020!

Don't miss it! Join the T. Kevin Bryan mailing list at

tkevinbryan.com

Made in the USA
San Bernardino, CA
21 December 2019

62155324R00175